The Shadow Kingdom

and

Other Tales

by

Robert E. Howard

Cover: Yellow Mountain, by Tom Thai, used under a Creative Commons Attribution 2.0 Generic license.

Printed on acid-free ANSI archival quality paper.

Contents

The Shadow Kingdom

1. A King Comes Riding

THE BLARE of the trumpets grew louder, like a deep golden tide surge, like the soft booming of the evening tides against the silver beaches of Valusia. The throng shouted, women flung roses from the roofs as the rhythmic chiming of silver hosts came clearer and the first of the mighty array swung into view in the broad white street that curved round the golden-spired Tower of Splendor.

First came the trumpeters, slim youths, clad in scarlet, riding with a flourish of long, slender golden trumpets; next the bowmen, tall men from the mountains; and behind these the heavily armed footmen, their broad shields clashing in unison, their long spears swaying in perfect rhythm to their stride. Behind them came the mightiest soldiery in all the world, the Red Slayers, horsemen, splendidly mounted, armed in red from helmet to spur. Proudly they sat their steeds, looking neither to right nor to left, but aware of the shouting for all that. Like bronze statues they were, and there was never a waver in the forest of spears that reared above them.

Behind those proud and terrible ranks came the motley files of the mercenaries, fierce, wild-looking warriors, men of Mu and of Kaa-u and of the hills of the east and the isles of the west. They bore spears and heavy swords, and a compact group that marched somewhat apart were the bowmen of Lemuria. Then came the light foot of the nation, and more trumpeters brought up the rear.

A brave sight, and a sight which aroused a fierce thrill in the soul of Kull, king of Valusia. Not on the Topaz Throne at the front of the regal Tower of Splendor sat Kull, but in the saddle, mounted on a great stallion, a true warrior king. His mighty arm swung up in reply to the salutes as the hosts passed. His fierce eyes passed the gorgeous trumpeters with a casual glance, rested longer on the following soldiery; they blazed with a ferocious light as the Red Slayers halted in front of him with a clang of arms and a rearing of steeds, and tendered him the crown salute. They narrowed slightly as the mercenaries strode by. They saluted no one, the mercenaries. They walked with shoulders flung back, eyeing Kull boldly and straightly, albeit with a certain appreciation; fierce eyes, unblinking; savage eyes, staring from beneath shaggy manes and heavy brows.

And Kull gave back a like stare. He granted much to brave men, and there were no braver in all the world, not even among the wild tribesmen who now disowned him. But Kull was too much the savage to have any great love for these. There were too many feuds. Many were age-old enemies of Kull's nation, and though the name of Kull was now a word accursed among the mountains and valleys of his people, and though Kull had put them from his mind, yet the old hates, the ancient passions still lingered. For Kull was no Valusian but an Atlantean.

The armies swung out of sight around the gemblazing shoulders of the Tower of Splendor and Kull reined his stallion about and started toward the palace at an easy gait, discussing the review with the commanders that rode with him, using not many words, but saying much.

"The army is like a sword," said Kull, "and must not be allowed to rust." So down the street they rode, and Kull gave no heed to any of the whispers that reached his hearing from the throngs that still swarmed the streets.

"That is Kull, see! Valka! But what a king! And what a man! Look at his arms! His shoulders!"

And an undertone of more sinister whispering:

"Kull! Ha, accursed usurper from the pagan isles." "Aye, shame to Valusia that a barbarian sits on the Throne of Kings."

Little did Kull heed. Heavy-handed had he seized the decaying throne of ancient Valusia and with a heavier hand did he hold it, a man against a nation.

After the council chamber, the social palace where Kull replied to the formal and laudatory phrases of the lords and ladies, with carefully hidden grim amusement at such frivolities; then the lords and ladies took their formal departure and Kull leaned back upon the ermine throne and contemplated matters of state until an attendant requested permission from the great king to speak, and announced an emissary from the Pictish embassy.

Kull brought his mind back from the dim mazes of Valusian statecraft where it had been wandering, and gazed upon the Pict with little favor. The man gave back the gaze of the king without flinching. He was a lean-hipped, massive-chested warrior of middle height, dark, like all his race, and strongly built. From strong, immobile features gazed dauntless and inscrutable eyes.

"The chief of the Councilors, Ka-nu of the tribe right hand of the king of Pictdom, sends greetings and says:" "There is a throne at the feast of the rising moon for Kull, king of kings, lord of lords, emperor of Valusia."

"Good," answered Kull. "Say to Ka-nu the Ancient, ambassador of the western isles, that the king of Valusia will quaff wine with him when the moon floats over the hills of Zalgara."

Still the Pict lingered. "I have a word for the king, not" – with a contemptuous flirt of his hand – "for these slaves."

Kull dismissed the attendants with a word, watching the Pict warily.

The man stepped nearer, and lowered his voice:

"Come alone to feast tonight, lord king. Such was the word of my chief."

The king's eyes narrowed, gleaming like gray sword steel, coldly.

"Alone?"

"Aye."

They eyed each other silently, their mutual tribal enmity seething beneath their cloak of formality. Their mouths spoke the cultured speech, the conventional court phrases of a highly polished race, a race not their own, but from their eyes gleamed the primal traditions of the elemental savage. Kull might be the king of Valusia and the Pict might be an emissary to her courts, but there in the throne hall of kings, two tribesmen glowered at each other, fierce and wary, while ghosts of wild wars and world-ancient feuds whispered to each.

To the king was the advantage and he enjoyed it to its fullest extent. Jaw resting on hand, he eyed the Pict, who stood like an image of bronze, head flung back, eyes unflinching.

Across Kull's lips stole a smile that was more a sneer.

"And so I am to come-alone?" Civilization had taught him to speak by innuendo and the Pict's dark eyes glittered, though he made no reply. "How am I to know that you come from Ka-nu?"

"I have spoken," was the sullen response.

"And when did a Pict speak truth?" sneered Kull, fully aware that the Picts never lied, but using this means to enrage the man.

"I see your plan, king," the Pict answered imperturbably. "You wish to anger me. By Valka, you need go no further! I am angry enough. And I challenge you to meet me in single battle, spear, sword or dagger, mounted or afoot. Are you king or man?"

Kull's eyes glinted with the grudging admiration a warrior must needs give a bold foeman, but he did not fail to use the chance of further annoying his antagonist.

"A king does not accept the challenge of a nameless savage," he sneered, "nor does the emperor of Valusia break the Truce of Ambassadors. You have leave to go. Say to Ka-nu I will come alone."

The Pict's eyes flashed murderously. He fairly shook in the grasp of the primitive blood-lust; then, turning his back squarely upon the king of Valusia, he strode across the Hall of Society and vanished through the great door.

Again Kull leaned back upon the ermine throne and meditated.

So the chief of the Council of Picts wished him to come alone? But for what reason? Treachery? Grimly Kull touched the hilt of his great sword. But scarcely. The Picts valued too greatly the alliance with Valusia to break it for any feudal reason. Kull might be a warrior of Atlantis and hereditary enemy of all Picts, but too, he was king of Valusia, the most potent ally of the Men of the West.

Kull reflected long upon the strange state of affairs that made him ally of ancient foes and foe of ancient friends. He rose and paced restlessly across the hall, with the quick, noiseless tread of a lion. Chains of friendship, tribe and tradition had he broken to satisfy his ambition. And, by Valka, god of the sea and the land, he had realized that ambition! He was king of Valusia-a fading, degenerate Valusia, a Valusia living mostly in dreams of bygone glory, but still a mighty land and the greatest of the Seven Empires. Valusia-Land of Dreams, the tribesmen named it, and sometimes it seemed to Kull that he moved in a dream. Strange to him were the intrigues of court and palace, army and people. All was like a masquerade, where men and women hid their real thoughts with a smooth mask. Yet the seizing of the throne had been easy-a bold snatching of opportunity, the swift whirl of swords, the slaying of a tyrant of whom men had wearied unto death, short, crafty plotting with ambitious statesmen out of favor at court-and Kull, wandering adventurer, Atlantean exile, had swept up to the dizzy heights of his dreams: he was lord of Valusia, king of kings. Yet now it seemed that the seizing was far easier than the keeping. The sight of the Pict had brought back youthful associations to his mind, the free, wild savagery of his boyhood. And now a strange feeling of dim unrest, of unreality, stole over him as of late it had been doing. Who was he, a straightforward man of the seas and the mountain, to rule a race strangely and terribly wise with the mysticisms of antiquity? An ancient race-

"I am Kull!" said he, flinging back his head as a lion flings back his mane. "I am Kull!"

His falcon gaze swept the ancient hall. His self-confidence flowed back. . . . And in a dim nook of the hall a tapestry moved-slightly.

2. Thus Spake the Silent Halls of Valusia

The moon had not risen, and the garden was lighted with torches aglow in silver cressets when Kull sat down on the throne before the table of Ka-nu, ambassador of the western isles. At his right hand sat the ancient Pict, as much unlike an emissary of that fierce race as a man could be. Ancient was Ka-nu and wise in statecraft, grown old in the game. There was no elemental hatred in the eyes that looked at Kull appraisingly; no Tribal traditions hindered his judgments. Long associations with the statesmen of the civilized nations had swept away such cobwebs. Not: who and what is this man? was the question ever foremost in Ka-nu's mind, but: can I use this man, and how? Tribal prejudices he used only to further his own schemes.

And Kull watched Ka-nu, answering his conversation briefly, wondering if civilization would make of him a thing like the Pict. For Ka-nu was soft and paunchy. Many years had stridden across the sky-rim since Ka-nu had wielded a sword. True, he was old, but Kull had seen men older than he in the forefront of battle. The Picts were a long-lived race. A beautiful girl stood at Ka-nu's elbow, refilling his goblet, and she was kept busy. Meanwhile Ka-nu kept up a running fire of jests and comments, and Kull, secretly contemptuous of his garrulity, nevertheless missed none of his shrewd humor.

At the banquet were Pictish chiefs and statesmen, the latter jovial and easy in their manner, the warriors formally courteous, but plainly hampered by their tribal affinities. Yet Kull, with a tinge of envy, was cognizant of the freedom and ease of the affair as contrasted with like affairs of the Valusian court. Such freedom prevailed in the rude camps of Atlantis-Kull shrugged his shoulders. After all, doubtless Ka-nu, who had seemed to have forgotten he was a Pict as far as time-hoary custom and prejudice went, was right and he, Kull, would better become a Valusian in mind as in name.

At last when the moon had reached her zenith, Ka-nu, having eaten and drunk as much as any three men there, leaned back upon his divan with a comfortable sigh and said, "Now, get you gone, friends, for the king and I would converse on such matters as concern not children. Yes, you too, my pretty; yet first let me kiss those ruby lips-so; no, dance away, my rose-bloom."

Ka-nu's eyes twinkled above his white beard as he surveyed Kull, who sat erect, grim and uncompromising.

"You are thinking, Kull," said the old statesman, suddenly, "that Ka-nu is a useless old reprobate, fit for nothing except to guzzle wine and kiss wenches!"

In fact, this remark was so much in line with his actual thoughts, and so plainly put, that Kull was rather startled, though he gave no sign.

Ka-nu gurgled and his paunch shook with his mirth. "Wine is red and women are soft," he remarked tolerantly. "But-ha! ha!-think not old Ka-nu allows either to interfere with business."

Again he laughed, and Kull moved restlessly. This seemed much like being made sport of, and the king's scintillant eyes began to glow with a feline light.

Ka-nu reached for the wine-pitcher, filled his beaker and glanced questioningly at Kull, who shook his head irritably.

"Aye," said Ka-nu equably, "it takes an old head to stand strong drink. I am growing old, Kull, so why should you young men begrudge me such pleasures as we oldsters must find? Ah me, I grow ancient and withered, friendless and cheerless."

But his looks and expressions failed far of bearing out his words. His rubicund countenance fairly glowed, and his eyes sparkled, so that his white beard seemed incongruous. Indeed, he looked remarkably elfin, reflected Kull, who felt vaguely resentful. The old scoundrel had lost all of the primitive virtues of his race and of Kull's race, yet he seemed more pleased in his aged days than otherwise.

"Hark ye, Kull," said Ka-nu, raising an admonitory finger, "'tis a chancy thing to laud a young man, yet I must speak my true thoughts to gain your confidence."

"If you think to gain it by flattery–"

"Tush. Who spake of flattery? I flatter only to disguard."

There was a keen sparkle in Ka-nu's eyes, a cold glimmer that did not match his lazy smile. He knew men, and he knew that to gain his end he must smite straight with this tigerish barbarian, who, like a wolf scenting a snare, would scent out unerringly any falseness in the skein of his wordweb.

"You have power, Kull," said he, choosing his words with more care than he did in the council rooms of the nation, "to make yourself mightiest of all kings, and restore some of the lost glories of Valusia. So. I care little for Valusia-though the women and wine be excellent-save for the fact that the stronger Valusia is, the stronger is the Pict nation. More, with an Atlantean on the throne, eventually Atlantis will become united–"

Kull laughed in harsh mockery. Ka-nu had touched an old wound.

"Atlantis made my name accursed when I went to seek fame and fortune among the cities of the world. We-they-are age-old foes of the Seven Empires, greater foes of the allies of the Empires, as you should know."

Ka-nu tugged his beard and smiled enigmatically.

"Nay, nay. Let it pass. But I know whereof I speak. And then warfare will cease, wherein there is no gain; I see a world of peace and prosperity-man loving his fellow man-the good supreme. All this can you accomplish-if you live!"

"Ha!" Kull's lean hand closed on his hilt and he half rose, with a sudden movement of such dynamic speed that Ka-nu, who fancied men as some men fancy blooded horses, felt his old blood leap with a sudden thrill. Valka, what a warrior! Nerves and sinews of steel and fire, bound together with the perfect co-ordination, the fighting instinct, that makes the terrible warrior.

But none of Ka-nu's enthusiasm showed in his mildly sarcastic tone.

"Tush. Be seated. Look about you. The gardens are deserted, the seats empty, save for ourselves. You fear not me?"

Kull sank back, gazing about him warily.

"There speaks the savage," mused Ka-nu. "Think you if I planned treachery I would enact it here where suspicion would be sure to fall upon me? Tut. You young tribesmen have much to learn. There were my chiefs who were not at ease because you were born among the hills of Atlantis, and you despise me in your secret mind because I am a Pict. Tush. I see you as Kull, king of Valusia, not as Kull, the reckless Atlantean, leader of the raiders who harried the western isles. So you should see in me, not a Pict but an international man, a figure of the world. Now to that figure, hark! If you were slain tomorrow who would be king?"

"Kaanuub, baron of Blaal."

"Even so. I object to Kaanuub for many reasons, yet most of all for the fact that he is but a figurehead."

"How so? He was my greatest opponent, but I did not know that he championed any cause but his own."

"The night can hear," answered Ka-nu obliquely. "There are worlds within worlds. But you may trust me and you may trust Brule, the Spear-slayer. Look!" He drew from his robes a bracelet of gold representing a winged dragon coiled thrice, with three horns of ruby on the head.

"Examine it closely. Brule will wear it on his arm when he comes to you tomorrow night so that you may know him. Trust Brule as you trust yourself, and do what he tells you to. And in proof of trust, look ye!"

And with the speed of a striking hawk, the ancient snatched something from his robes, something that flung a weird green light over them, and which he replaced in an instant.

"The stolen gem!" exclaimed Kull recoiling. "The green jewel from the Temple of the Serpent! Valka! You! And why do you show it to me?"

"To save your life. To prove my trust. If I betray your trust, deal with me likewise. You hold my life in your hand. Now I could not be false to you if I would, for a word from you would be my doom."

Yet for all his words the old scoundrel beamed merrily and seemed vastly pleased with himself.

"But why do you give me this hold over you?" asked Kull, becoming more bewildered each second.

"As I told you. Now, you see that I do not intend to deal you false, and tomorrow night when Brule comes to you, you will follow his advice without fear of treachery. Enough. An escort waits outside to ride to the palace with you, lord."

Kull rose. "But you have told me nothing."

"Tush. How impatient are youths!" Ka-nu looked more like a mischievous elf than ever. "Go you and dream of thrones and power and kingdoms, while I dream of wine and soft women and roses. And fortune ride with you, King Kull."

As he left the garden, Kull glanced back to see Ka-nu still reclining lazily in his seat, a merry ancient, beaming on all the world with jovial fellowship.

A mounted warrior waited for the king Just without the garden and Kull was slightly surprised to see that it was the same that had brought Ka-nu's invitation. No word was spoken as Kull swung into the saddle nor as they clattered along the empty streets.

The color and the gayety of the day had given way to the eerie stillness of night. The city's antiquity was more than ever apparent beneath the bent, silver moon. The huge pillars of the mansions and palaces towered up into the stars. The broad stairways, silent and deserted, seemed to climb endlessly until they vanished in the shadowy darkness of the upper realms. Stairs to the stars, thought Kull, his imaginative mind inspired by the weird grandeur of the scene.

Clang! clang! clang! sounded the silver hoofs on the broad, moon-flooded streets, but otherwise there was no sound. The age of the city, its incredible antiquity, was almost oppressive to the king; it was as if the great silent buildings laughed at him, noiselessly, with unguessable mockery. And what secrets did they hold?

"You are young," said the palaces and the temples and the shrines, "but we are old. The world was wild with youth when we were reared. You and your tribe shall pass, but we are invincible, indestructible. We towered above a strange world, ere Atlantis and Lemuria rose from the sea; we still shall reign when the green waters sigh for many a restless fathom above the spires of Lemuria and the hills of Atlantis and when the isles of the Western Men are the mountains of a strange land.

"How many kings have we watched ride down these streets before Kull of Atlantis was even a dream in the mind of Ka, bird of Creation? Ride on, Kull of Atlantis; greater shall follow you; greater came before you. They are dust; they are forgotten; we stand; we know; we are. Ride, ride on, Kull of Atlantis; Kull the king, Kull the fool!"

And it seemed to Kull that the clashing hoofs took up the silent refrain to beat it into the night with hollow re-echoing mockery; "Kull-the-king! Kull-the-fool!"

Glow, moon; you light a king's way! Gleam, stars; you are torches in the train of an emperor! And clang, silver-shod hoofs; you herald that Kull rides through Valusia.

Ho! Awake, Valusia! It is Kull that rides, Kull the king!

"We have known many kings," said the silent halls of Valusia.

And so in a brooding mood Kull came to the palace, where his bodyguard, men of the Red Slayers, came to take the rein of the great stallion and escort Kull to his rest. There the Pict, still sullenly speechless, wheeled his steed with a savage wrench of the rein and fled away in the dark like a phantom; Kull's heightened imagination pictured him speeding through the silent streets like a goblin out of the Elder World.

There was no sleep for Kull that night, for it was nearly dawn and he spent the rest of the night hours pacing the throne-room, and pondering over what had passed. Ka-nu had told him nothing, yet he had put himself in Kull's complete power. At what had he hinted when he had said the baron of Blaal was naught but a figurehead? And who was this Brule who was to come to him by night, wearing the mystic armlet of the dragon? And why? Above all, why had Ka-nu shown him the green gem of terror, stolen long ago from the temple of the Serpent, for which the world would rock in wars were it known to the weird and terrible keepers of that temple, and from whose vengeance not even Ka-nu's ferocious tribesmen might be able to save him? But Ka-nu knew he was safe, reflected Kull, for the statesman was too shrewd to expose himself to risk without profit. But was it to throw the king off his guard and pave the way to treachery? Would Ka-nu dare let him live now? Kull shrugged his shoulders.

3. They That Walk the Night

The moon had not risen when Kull, hand to hilt, stepped to a window. The windows opened upon the great inner gardens of the royal palace, and the breezes of the night, bearing the scents of spice trees, blew the filmy curtains about. The king looked out. The walks and groves were deserted; carefully trimmed trees were bulky shadows; fountains near by flung their slender sheen of silver in the starlight and distant fountains rippled steadily. No guards walked those gardens, for so closely were the outer walls guarded that it seemed impossible for any invader to gain access to them.

Vines curled up the walls of the palace, and even as Kull mused upon the ease with which they might be climbed, a segment of shadow detached itself from the darkness below the window and a bare, brown arm curved up over the sill. Kull's great sword hissed halfway from the sheath; then the King halted. Upon the muscular forearm gleamed the dragon armlet shown him by Ka-nu the night before.

The possessor of the arm pulled himself up over the sill and into the room with the swift, easy motion of a climbing leopard.

"You are Brule?" asked Kull, and then stopped in surprise not unmingled with annoyance and suspicion; for the man was he whom Kull had taunted in the Hall of Society; the same who had escorted him from the Pictish embassy.

"I am Brule, the Spear-slayer," answered the Pict in a guarded voice; then swiftly, gazing closely in Kull's face, he said, barely above a whisper:

"Ka nama kaa lajerama!"

Kull started. "Ha! What mean you?"

"Know you not?"

"Nay, the words are unfamiliar; they are of no language I ever heard-and yet, by Valka!-somewhere-I have heard–"

"Aye," was the Pict's only comment. His eyes swept the room, the study room of the palace. Except for a few tables, a divan or two and great shelves of books of parchment, the room was barren compared to the grandeur of the rest of the palace.

"Tell me, king, who guards the door?"

"Eighteen of the Red Slayers. But how come you, stealing through the gardens by night and scaling the walls of the palace?"

Brule sneered. "The guards of Valusia are blind buffaloes. I could steal their girls from under their noses. I stole amid them and they saw me not nor heard me. And the walls-I could scale them without the aid of vines. I have hunted tigers on the foggy beaches when the sharp east breezes blew the mist in from seaward and I have climbed the steeps of the western sea mountain. But come-nay, touch this armlet."

He held out his arm and, as Kull complied wonderingly, gave an apparent sigh of relief.

"So. Now throw off those kingly robes; for there are ahead of you this night such deeds as no Atlantean ever dreamed of."

Brule himself was clad only in a scanty loin-cloth through which was thrust a short, curved sword.

"And who are you to give me orders?" asked Kull, slightly resentful.

"Did not Ka-nu bid you follow me in all things?" asked the Pict irritably, his eyes flashing momentarily. "I have no love for you, lord, but for the moment I have put the thought of feuds from my mind. Do you likewise. But come."

Walking noiselessly, he led the way across the room to the door. A slide in the door allowed a view of the outer corridor, unseen from without, and the Pict bade Kull look.

"What see you?"

"Naught but the eighteen guardsmen."

The Pict nodded, motioned Kull to follow him across the room. At a panel in the opposite wall Brule stopped and fumbled there a moment. Then with a light movement he stepped back, drawing his sword as he did so. Kull gave an exclamation as the panel swung silently open, revealing a dimly lighted passageway.

"A secret passage!" swore Kull softly. "And I knew nothing or it! By Valka, someone shall dance for this!"

"Silence!" hissed the Pict.

Brule was standing like a bronze statue as if straining every nerve for the slightest sound; something about his attitude made Kull's hair prickle slightly, not from fear but from some eerie anticipation. Then beckoning, Brule stepped through the secret doorway which stood open behind them. The passage was bare, but not dust-covered as should have been the case with an unused secret corridor. A vague, gray light filtered through somewhere, but the source of it was not apparent. Every few feet Kull saw doors, invisible, as he knew, from the outside, but easily apparent from within.

"The palace is a very honeycomb," he muttered. "Aye. Night and day you are watched, king, by many eyes."

The king was impressed by Brule's manner. The Pict went forward slowly, warily, half crouching, blade held low and thrust forward. When he spoke it was in a whisper and he continually flung glances from side to side.

The corridor turned sharply and Brule warily gazed past the turn.

"Look!" he whispered. "But remember! No word! No sound-on your life!"

Kull cautiously gazed past him. The corridor changed just at the bend to a flight of steps. And then Kull recoiled. At the foot of those stairs lay the eighteen Red Slayers who were that night stationed to watch the long's study room. Brule's grip upon his mighty arm and Brule's fierce whisper at his shoulder alone kept Kull from leaping down those stairs.

"Silent, Kull! Silent, in Valka's name!" hissed the Pict. "These corridors are empty now, but I risked much in showing you, that you might then believe what I had to say. Back now to the room of study." And he retraced his steps, Kull following; his mind in a turmoil of bewilderment.

"This is treachery," muttered the long, his steel gray eyes a-smolder, "foul and swift! Mere minutes have passed since those men stood at guard."

Again in the room of study Brule carefully closed the secret panel and motioned Kull to look again through the slit of the outer door. Kull gasped audibly. For without stood the eighteen guardsmen!

"This is sorcery!" he whispered, half-drawing his sword. "Do dead men guard the long?"

"Aye!" came Brule's scarcely audible reply; there was a strange expression in the Pict's scintillant eyes. They looked squarely into each other's eyes for an instant, Kull's brow wrinkled in a puzzled scowl as he strove to read the Pict's inscrutable face. Then Brule's lips, barely moving, formed the words; "The-snake-that-speaks!".

"Silent!" whispered Kull, laying his hand over Brule's mouth. "That is death to speak! That is a name accursed!"

The Pict's fearless eyes regarded him steadily.

"Look, again. King Kull. Perchance the guard was changed."

"Nay, those are the same men. In Valka's name, this is sorcery-this is insanity! I saw with my own eyes the bodies of those men, not eight minutes agone. Yet there they stand."

Brule stepped back, away from the door, Kull mechanically following.

"Kull, what know ye of the traditions of this race ye rule?"

"Much-and yet, little. Valusia is so old–" "Aye," Brule's eyes lighted strangely, "we are but barbarians-infants compared to the Seven Empires. Not even they themselves know how old they are. Neither the memory of man nor the annals of the historians reach back far enough to tell us when the first men came up from the sea and built cities on the shore. But Kull, men were not always ruled by men!" The king started. Their eyes met. "Aye, there is a legend of my people" – "And mine!" broke in Brule. "That was before we of the isles were allied with Valusia. Aye, in the reign of Lion-fang, seventh war chief of the Picts, so many years ago no man remembers how many. Across the sea we came, from the isles of the sunset, skirting the shores of Atlantis, and falling upon the beaches of Valusia with fire and sword. Aye, the long white beaches resounded with the clash of spears, and the night was like day from the flame of the burning castles.

And the king, the king of Valusia, who died on the red sea sands that dim day–" His voice trailed off; the two stared at each other, neither speaking; then each nodded.

"Ancient is Valusia!" whispered Kull. "The hills of Atlantis and Mu were isles of the sea when Valusia was young."

The night breeze whispered through the open window. Not the free, crisp sea air such as Brule and Kull knew and reveled in, in their land, but a breath like a whisper from the past, laden with musk, scents of forgotten things, breathing secrets that were hoary when the world was young.

The tapestries rustled, and suddenly Kull felt like a naked child before the inscrutable wisdom of the mystic past. Again the sense of unreality swept upon him. At the back of his soul stole dim, gigantic phantoms, whispering monstrous things. He sensed that Brule experienced similar thoughts. The Pict's eyes were fixed upon his face with a fierce intensity. Their glances met. Kull felt warmly a sense of comradeship with this member of an enemy tribe. Like rival leopards turning at bay against hunters, these two savages made common cause against the inhuman powers of antiquity. Brule again led the way back to the secret door. Silently they entered and silently they proceeded down the dim corridor, taking the opposite direction from that in which they previously traversed it. After a while the Pict stopped and pressed close to one of the secret doors, bidding Kull look with him through the hidden slot.

"This opens upon a little-used stair which leads to a corridor running past the study-room door."

They gazed, and presently, mounting the stair silently, came a silent shape.

"Tu! Chief councilor!" exclaimed Kull. "By night and with bared dagger! How, what means this, Brule?"

"Murder! And foulest treachery!" hissed Brule. "Nay" – as Kull would have flung the door aside and leaped forth – "we are lost if you meet him here, for more lurk at the foot of those stairs. Come!"

Half running, they darted back along the passage. Back through the secret door Brule led, shutting it carefully behind them, then across the chamber to an opening into a room seldom used. There he swept aside some tapestries in a dim corner nook and, drawing Kull with him, stepped behind them. Minutes dragged. Kull could hear the breeze in the other room blowing the window curtains about, and it seemed to him like the murmur of ghosts. Then through the door, stealthily, came Tu, chief councilor of the king. Evidently he had come through the study room and, finding it empty, sought his victim where he was most likely to be.

He came with upraised dagger, walking silently. A moment he halted, gazing about the apparently empty room, which was lighted dimly by a single candle. Then he advanced cautiously, apparently at a loss to understand the absence of the king. He stood before the hiding place-and "Slay!" hissed the Pict.

Kull with a single mighty leap hurled himself into the room. Tu spun, but the blinding, tigerish speed of the attack gave him no chance for defense or counterattack. Sword steel flashed in the dim light and grated on bone as Tu toppled backward, Kull's sword standing out between his shoulders.

Kull leaned above him, teeth bared in the killer's snarl, heavy brows ascowl above eyes that were like the gray ice of the cold sea. Then he released the hilt and recoiled, shaken, dizzy, the hand of death at his spine.

For as he watched, Tu's face became strangely dim and unreal; the features mingled and merged in a seemingly impossible manner. Then, like a fading mask of fog, the face suddenly vanished and in its stead gaped and leered a monstrous serpent's head! "Valka!" gasped Kull, sweat beading his forehead, and again; "Valka!"

Brule leaned forward, face immobile. Yet his glittering eyes mirrored something of Kull's horror.

"Regain your sword, lord king," said he. "There are yet deeds to be done."

Hesitantly Kull set his hand to the hilt. His flesh crawled as he set his foot upon the terror which lay at their feet, and as some jerk of muscular reaction caused the frightful mouth to gape suddenly, he recoiled, weak with nausea. Then, wrathful at himself, he plucked forth his sword and gazed more closely at the nameless thing that had been known as Tu, chief councilor. Save for the reptilian head, the thing was the exact counterpart of a man.

"A man with the head of a snake!" Kull murmured. "This, then, is a priest of the serpent god?"

"Aye. Tu sleeps unknowing. These fiends can take any form they will. That is, they can, by a magic charm or the like, fling a web of sorcery about their faces, as an actor dons a mask, so that they resemble anyone they wish to."

"Then the old legends were true," mused the king; "the grim old tales few dare even whisper, lest they die as blasphemers, are no fantasies. By Valka, I had thought-I had guessed-but it seems beyond the bounds of reality. Ha! The guardsmen outside the door–"

"They too are snake-men. Hold! What would you do?"

"Slay them!" said Kull between his teeth.

"Strike at the skull if at all," said Brule. "Eighteen wait without the door and perhaps a score more in the corridors. Hark ye, king, Ka-nu learned of this plot. His spies have pierced the inmost fastnesses of the snake priests and they brought hints of a plot. Long ago he discovered the secret passageways of the palace, and at his command I studied the map thereof and came here by night to aid you, lest you die as other kings of Valusia have died. I came alone for the reason that to send more would have roused suspicion. Many could not steal into the palace as I did. Some of the foul conspiracy you have seen. Snake-men guard your door, and that one, as Tu, could pass anywhere else in the palace; in the morning, if the priests failed, the real guards would be holding their places again, nothing knowing, nothing remembering; there to take the blame if the priests succeeded. But stay you here while I dispose of this carrion."

So saying, the Pict shouldered the frightful thing stolidly and vanished with it through another secret panel.

Kull stood alone, his mind a-whirl. Neophytes of the mighty serpent, how many lurked among his cities? How might he tell the false from the true? Aye, how many of his trusted councilors, his generals, were men? He could be certain-of whom?

The secret panel swung inward and Brule entered.

"You were swift."

"Aye!" The warrior stepped forward, eyeing the floor. "There is gore upon the rug. See?"

Kull bent forward; from the corner of his eye he saw a blur of movement, a glint of steel. Like a loosened bow he whipped erect, thrusting upward. The warrior sagged upon the sword, his own clattering to the floor. Even at that instant Kull reflected grimly that it was appropriate that the traitor should meet his death upon the sliding, upward thrust used so much by his race. Then, as Brule slid from the sword to sprawl motionless on the floor, the face began to merge and fade, and as Kull caught his breath, his hair a-prickle, the human features vanished and there the jaws of a great snake gaped hideously, the terrible beady eyes venomous even in death.

"He was a snake priest all the time!" gasped the king. "Valka! What an elaborate plan to throw me off my guard! Ka-nu there, is he a man? Was it Ka-nu to whom I talked in the gardens? Almighty Valka!" as his flesh crawled with a horrid thought; "are the people of Valusia men or are they all serpents?"

Undecided he stood, idly seeing that the thing named Brule no longer wore the dragon armlet. A sound made him wheel.

Brute was coming through the secret door.

"Hold!" Upon the arm upthrown to halt the king's hovering sword gleamed the dragon armlet. "Valka!" The Pict stopped short. Then a grim smile curled his lips.

"By the gods of the seas! These demons are crafty past reckoning. For it must be that one lurked in the corridors, and seeing me go carrying the carcass of that other, took my appearance. So. I have another to do away with."

"Hold!" there was the menace of death in Kull's voice; "I have seen two men turn to serpents before my eyes. How may I know if you are a true man?"

Brule laughed. "For two reasons. King Kull. No snake-man wears this" – he indicated the dragon armlet – "nor can any say these words," and again Kull heard the strange phrase; "Ka nama kaa lajerama."

"Ka nama kaa lajerama" Kull repeated mechanically. "Now, where, in Valka's name, have I heard that? I have not! And yet– and yet–"

"Aye, you remember, Kull," said Brule. "Through the dim corridors of memory those words lurk; though you never heard them in this life, yet in the bygone ages they were so terribly impressed upon the soul mind that never dies, that they will always strike dim chords in your memory, though you be reincarnated for a million years to come. For that phrase has come secretly down the grim and bloody eons, since when, uncounted centuries ago, those words were watchwords for the race of men who battled with the grisly beings of the Elder Universe. For none but a real man of men may speak them, whose jaws and mouth are shaped different from any other creature. Their meaning has been forgotten but not the words themselves."

"True," said Kull. "I remember the legends Valka!" He stopped short, staring, for suddenly, like the silent swinging wide of a mystic door, misty, unfathomed reaches opened in the recesses of his consciousness and for an instant he seemed to gaze back through the vastness that spanned life and life; seeing through the vague and ghostly fogs dim shapes reliving dead centuries-men in combat with hideous monsters, vanquishing a planet of frightful terrors. Against a gray, ever-shifting background moved strange nightmare forms, fantasies of lunacy and fear; and man, the jest of the gods, the blind, wisdom-less striver from dust to dust, following the long bloody trail of his destiny, knowing not why, bestial, blundering, like a great murderous child, yet feeling somewhere a spark of divine fire . . . Kull drew a hand across his brow, shaken; these sudden glimpses into the abysses of memory always startled him.

"They are gone," said Brule, as if scanning his secret mind; "the bird-women, the harpies, the bat-men, the flying fiends, the wolf-people, the demons, the goblins-all save such as this being that lies at our feet, and a few of the wolf-men. Long and terrible was the war, lasting through the bloody centuries, since first the first men, risen from the mire of apedom, turned upon those who then ruled the world."

"And at last mankind conquered, so long ago that naught but dim legends come to us through the ages. The snake-people were the last to go, yet at last men conquered even them and drove them forth into the waste lands of the world, there to mate with true snakes until some day, say the sages, the horrid breed shall vanish utterly. Yet the Things returned in crafty guise as men grew soft and degenerate, forgetting ancient wars. Ah, that was a grim and secret war! Among the men of the Younger Earth stole the frightful monsters of the Elder Planet, safeguarded by their horrid wisdom and mysticisms, taking all forms and shapes, doing deeds of horror secretly. No man knew who was true man and who false. No man could trust any man. Yet by means of their own craft they formed ways by which the false might be known from the true. Men took for a sign and a standard the figure of the flying dragon, the winged dinosaur, a monster of past ages, which was the greatest foe of the serpent. And men used those words which I spoke to you as a sign and symbol, for as I said, none but a true man can repeat them. So mankind triumphed. Yet again the fiends came after the years of forgetfulness had gone by-for man is still an ape in that he forgets what is not ever before his eyes. As priests they came; and for that men in their luxury and might had by then lost faith in the old religions and worships, the snake-men, in the guise of teachers of a new and truer cult, built a monstrous religion about the worship of the serpent god. Such is their power that it is now death to repeat the old legends of the snake-people, and people bow again to the serpent god in new form; and blind fools that they are, the great hosts of men see no connection between this power and the power men overthrew eons ago. As priests the snake-men are content to rule – and yet–" He stopped.

"Go on." Kull felt an unaccountable stirring of the short hair at the base of his scalp.

"Kings have reigned as true men in Valusia," the Pict whispered, "and yet, slain in battle, have died serpents-as died he who fell beneath the spear of Lionfang on the red beaches when we of the isles harried the Seven Empires. And how can this be. Lord Kull? These kings were born of women and lived as men! This-the true kings died in secret-as you would have died tonight-and priests of the Serpent reigned in their stead, no man knowing."

Kull cursed between his teeth. "Aye, it must be. No one has ever seen a priest of the Serpent and lived, that is known. They live in utmost secrecy."

"The statecraft of the Seven Empires is a mazy, monstrous thing," said Brule. "There the true men know that among them glide the spies of the Serpent, and the men who are the Serpent's allies-such as Kaanuub, baron of Blaal-yet no man dares seek to unmask a suspect lest vengeance befall him. No man trusts his fellow and the true statesmen dare not speak to each other what is in the minds of all. Could they be sure, could a snake-man or plot be unmasked before them all, then would the power of the Serpent be more than half broken; for all would then ally and make common cause, sifting out the traitors. Ka-nu alone is of sufficient shrewdness and courage to cope with them, and even Ka-nu learned only enough of their plot to tell me what would happen-what has happened up to this time. Thus far I was prepared; from now on we must trust to our luck and our craft. Here and now I think we are safe; those snake-men without the door dare not leave their post lest true men come here unexpectedly. But tomorrow they will try something else, you may be sure. Just what they will do, none can say, not even Ka-nu; but we must stay at each other's sides. King Kull, until we conquer or both be dead. Now come with me while I take this carcass to the hiding-place where I took the other being."

Kull followed the Pict with his grisly burden through the secret panel and down the dim corridor. Their feet, trained to the silence of the wilderness, made no noise. Like phantoms they glided through the ghostly light, Kull wondering that the corridors should be deserted; at every turn he expected to run full upon some frightful apparition. Suspicion surged back upon him; was this Pict leading him into ambush? He fell back a pace or two behind Brule, his ready sword hovering at the Pict's unheeding back. Brule should die first if he meant treachery. But if the Pict was aware of the king's suspicion, he showed no sign. Stolidly he tramped along, until they came to a room, dusty and long unused, where moldy tapestries hung heavy. Brule drew aside some of these and concealed the corpse behind them.

Then they turned to retrace their steps, when suddenly Brule halted with such abruptness that he was closer to death than he knew; for Kull's nerves were on edge.

"Something moving in the corridor," hissed the Pict. "Ka-nu said these ways would be empty, yet–"

He drew his sword and stole into the corridor, Kull following warily.

A short way down the corridor a strange, vague glow appeared that came toward them. Nerves a-leap, they waited, backs to the corridor wall; for what they knew not, but Kull heard Brule's breath hiss through his teeth and was reassured as to Brule's loyalty.

The glow merged into a shadowy form. A shape vaguely like a man it was, but misty and illusive, like a wisp of fog, that grew more tangible as it approached, but never fully material A face looked at them, a pair of luminous great eyes, that seemed to hold all me tortures of a million centuries. There was no menace in that face, with its dim, worn features, but only a great pity-and that face-that face-

"Almighty gods!" breathed Kull, an icy hand at his soul; "Eallal, king of Valusia, who died a thousand years ago!"

Brule shrank back as far as he could, his narrow eyes widened in a blaze of pure horror, the sword shaking in his grip, unnerved for the first time that weird night. Erect and defiant stood Kull, instinctively holding his useless sword at the ready; flesh acrawl, hair a-prickle, yet still a king of kings, as ready to challenge the powers of the unknown dead as the powers of the living.

The phantom came straight on, giving them no heed; Kull shrank back as it passed them, feeling an icy breath like a breeze from the arctic snow. Straight on went the shape with slow, silent footsteps, as if the chains of all the ages were upon those vague feet; vanishing about a bend of the corridor.

"Valka!" muttered the Pict, wiping the cold beads from his brow; "that was no man! That was a ghost!"

"Aye!" Kull shook his head wonderingly. "Did you not recognize the face? That was Eallal, who reigned in Valusia a thousand years ago and who was found hideously murdered in his throne-room-the room now known as the Accursed Room. Have you not seen his statue in the Fame Room of Kings?"

"Yes, I remember the tale now. Gods, Kull! that is another sign of the frightful and foul power of the snake priests-that king was slain by snake-people and thus his soul became their slave, to do their bidding throughout eternity! For the sages have ever maintained that if a man is slain by a snake-man his ghost becomes their slave."

A shudder shook Kull's gigantic frame. "Valka! But what a fate! Hark ye" – his fingers closed upon Brule's sinewy arm like steel – "hark ye! If I am wounded unto death by these foul monsters, swear that ye will smite your sword through my breast lest my soul be enslaved."

"I swear," answered Brule, his fierce eyes lighting. "And do ye the same by me, Kull."

Their strong right hands met in a silent sealing of their bloody bargain.

4. Masks

Kull sat upon his throne and gazed broodily out upon the sea of faces turned toward him. A courtier was speaking in evenly modulated tones, but the king scarcely heard him. Close by, Tu, chief councilor, stood ready at Kull's command, and each time the king looked at him, Kull shuddered inwardly. The surface of court life was as the unrippled surface of the sea between tide and tide. To the musing king the affairs of the night before seemed as a dream, until his eyes dropped to the arm of his throne. A brown, sinewy hand rested there, upon the wrist of which gleamed a dragon armlet; Brule stood beside his throne and ever the Pict's fierce secret whisper brought him back from the realm of unreality in which he moved.

No, that was no dream, that monstrous interlude. As he sat upon his throne in the Hall of Society and gazed upon the courtiers, the ladies, the lords, the statesmen, he seemed to see their faces as things of illusion, things unreal, existent only as shadows and mockeries of substance. Always he had seen their faces as masks, but before he had looked on them with contemptuous tolerance, thinking to see beneath the masks shallow, puny souls, avaricious, lustful, deceitful; now there was a grim undertone, a sinister meaning, a vague horror that lurked beneath the smooth masks. While he exchanged courtesies with some nobleman or councilor he seemed to see the smiling face fade like smoke and the frightful jaws of a serpent gaping there. How many of those he looked upon were horrid, inhuman monsters, plotting his death, beneath the smooth mesmeric illusion of a human face?

Valusia-land of dreams and nightmares-a kingdom of the shadows, ruled by phantoms who glided back and forth behind the painted curtains, mocking the futile king who sat upon the throne-himself a shadow.

And like a comrade shadow Brule stood by his side, dark eyes glittering from immobile face. A real man, Brule! And Kull felt his friendship for the savage become a thing of reality and sensed that Brule felt a friendship for him beyond the mere necessity of statecraft.

And what, mused Kull, were the realities of life? Ambition, power, pride? The friendship of man, the love of women-which Kull had never known-battle, plunder, what? Was it the real Kull who sat upon the throne or was it the real Kull who had scaled the hills of Atlantis, harried the far isles of the sunset, and laughed upon the green roaring tides of the Atlantean sea? How could a man be so many different men in a lifetime? For Kull knew that there were many Kulls and he wondered which was the real Kull. After all, the priests of the Serpent went a step further in their magic, for all men wore masks, and many a different mask with each different man or woman; and Kull wondered if a serpent did not lurk under every mask. So he sat and brooded in strange, mazy thought ways, and the courtiers came and went and the minor affairs of the day were completed, until at last the king and Brule sat alone in the Hall of Society save for the drowsy attendants.

Kull felt a weariness. Neither he nor Brule had slept the night before, nor had Kull slept the night before that, when in the gardens of Ka-nu he had had his first hint of the weird things to be. Last night nothing further had occurred after they had returned to the study room from the secret corridors, but they had neither dared nor cared to sleep. Kull, with the incredible vitality of a wolf, had aforetime gone for days upon days without sleep, in his wild savage days but now his mind was edged from constant thinking and from the nerve-breaking eeriness of the past night. He needed sleep, but sleep was furthest from his mind.

And he would not have dared sleep if he had thought of it. Another thing that had shaken him was the fact that though he and Brule had kept a close watch to see if, or when, the study-room guard was changed, yet it was changed without their knowledge; for the next morning those who stood on guard were able to repeat the magic words of Brule, but they remembered nothing out of the ordinary. They thought that they had stood at guard all night, as usual, and Kull said nothing to the contrary. He believed them true men, but Brule had advised absolute secrecy, and Kull also thought it best.

Now Brule leaned over the throne, lowering his voice so not even a lazy attendant could hear: "They will strike soon, I think, Kull. A while ago Ka-nu gave me a secret sign. The priests know that we know of their plot, of course, but they know not, how much we know. We must be ready for any sort of action. Ka-nu and the Pictish chiefs will remain within hailing distance now until this is settled one way or another. Ha, Kull, if it comes to a pitched battle, the streets and the castles of Valusia will run red!"

Kull smiled grimly. He would greet any sort of action with a ferocious joy. This wandering in a labyrinth of illusion and magic was extremely irksome to his nature. He longed for the leap and clang of swords, for the joyous freedom of battle.

Then into the Hall of Society came Tu again, and the rest of the councilors.

"Lord king, the hour of the council is at hand and we stand ready to escort you to the council room."

Kull rose, and the councilors bent the knee as he passed through the way opened by them for his passage, rising behind him, and following. Eyebrows were raised as the Pict strode defiantly behind the king, but no one dissented.

Brule's challenging gaze swept the smooth faces of the councilors with the defiance of an intruding savage.

The group passed through the halls and came at last to the council chamber. The door was closed, as usual, and the councilors arranged themselves in the order of their rank before the dais upon which stood the king. Like a bronze statue Brule took up his stand behind Kull.

Kull swept the room with a swift stare. Surely no chance of treachery here. Seventeen councilors there were, all known to him; all of them had espoused his cause when he ascended the throne.

"Men of Valusia–" he began in the conventional manner, then halted, perplexed. The councilors had risen as a man and were moving toward him. There was no hostility in their looks, but their actions were strange for a council room. The foremost was close to him when Brule sprang forward, crouched like a leopard.

"Ka. nama. kaa lajerama!" his voice crackled through the sinister silence of the room and the foremost councilor recoiled, hand flashing to his robes; and like a spring released, Brule moved and the man pitched headlong and lay still while his face faded and became the head of a mighty snake.

"Slay, Kull!" rasped the Pict's voice. "They be all serpent men!"

The rest was a scarlet maze. Kull saw the familiar faces dim like fading fog and in their places gaped horrid reptilian visages as the whole band rushed forward. His mind was dazed but his giant body faltered not.

The singing of his sword filled the room, and the onrushing flood broke in a red wave. But they surged forward again, seemingly willing to fling their lives away in order to drag down the king. Hideous jaws gaped at him; terrible eyes blazed into his unblinkingly; a frightful fetid scent pervaded the atmosphere-the serpent scent that Kull had known in southern jungles. Swords and daggers leaped at him and he was dimly aware that they wounded him. But Kull was in his element; never before had he faced such grim foes but it mattered little; they lived, their veins held blood that could be spilt and they died when his great sword cleft their skulls or drove through their bodies. Slash, thrust, thrust and swing. Yet had Kull died there but for the man who crouched at his side, parrying and thrusting. For the king was clear berserk, fighting in the terrible Atlantean way, that seeks death to deal death; he made no effort to avoid thrusts and slashes, standing straight up and ever plunging forward, no thought in his frenzied mind but to slay. Not often did Kull forget his fighting craft in his primitive fury, but now some chain had broken in his soul, flooding his mind with a red wave of slaughter-lust. He slew a foe at each blow, but they surged about him, and time and again Brule turned a thrust that would have slain, as he crouched beside Kull, parrying and warding with cold skill, slaying not as Kull slew with long slashes and plunges, but with short overhand blows and upward thrusts.

Kull laughed, a laugh of insanity. The frightful faces swirled about him in a scarlet blaze. He felt steel sink into his arm and dropped his sword in a flashing arc that cleft his foe to the breast-bone. Then the mists faded and the king saw that he and Brule stood alone above a sprawl of hideous crimson figures who lay still upon the floor.

"Valka! what a killing!" said Brule, shaking the blood from his eyes. "Kull, had these been warriors who knew how to use the steel, we had died here. These serpent priests know naught of swordcraft and die easier than any men I ever slew. Yet had there been a few more, I think the matter had ended otherwise."

Kull nodded. The wild berserker blaze had passed, leaving a mazed feeling of great weariness. Blood seeped from wounds on breast, shoulder, arm and leg. Brule, himself bleeding from a score of flesh wounds, glanced at him in some concern.

"Lord Kull, let us hasten to have your wounds dressed by the women."

Kull thrust him aside with a drunken sweep of his mighty arm.

"Nay, we'll see this through ere we cease. Go you, though, and have your wounds seen to-I command it."

The Pict laughed grimly. "Your wounds are more than mine, lord king–" he began, then stopped as a sudden thought struck him. "By Valka, Kull, this is not the council room!"

Kull looked about and suddenly other fogs seemed to fade. "Nay, this is the room where Eallal died a thousand years ago-since unused and named 'Accursed.'"

"Then by the gods, they tricked us after all!" exclaimed Brule in a fury, kicking the corpses at their feet.

"They caused us to walk like fools into their ambush! By their magic they changed the appearance of all–"

"Then there is further deviltry afoot." said Kull, "for if there be true men in the councils of Valusia they should be in the real council room now. Come swiftly."

And leaving the room with its ghastly keepers they hastened through halls that seemed deserted until they came to the real council room. Then Kull halted with a ghastly shudder. From the council room sounded a voice speaking, and the voice was his!

With a hand that shook he parted the tapestries and gazed into the room. There sat the councilors, counterparts of the men he and Brule had just slain, and upon the dais stood Kull, king of Valusia..

He stepped back, his mind reeling.

"This is insanity!" he whispered. "Am I Kull? Do I stand here or is that Kull yonder in very truth, arid am I but a shadow, a figment of thought?"

Brule's hand clutching his shoulder, shaking him fiercely, brought him to his senses.

"Valka's name, be not a fool! Can you yet be astounded after all we have seen? See you not that those are true men bewitched by a snake-man who has taken your form, as those others took their forms? By now you should have been slain, and yon monster reigning in your stead, unknown by those who bowed to you. Leap arid slay swiftly or else we are undone. The Red Slayers, true men, stand close on each hand and none but you can reach and slay him. Be swift!"

Kull shook off the onrushing dizziness, flung back his head in the old, defiant gesture. He took a long, deep breath as does a strong swimmer before diving into the sea; then, sweeping back the tapestries, made the dais in a single lion-like bound. Brule had spoken truly. There stood men of the Red Slavers, guardsmen trained to move quick as the striking leopard; any but Kull had died ere he could reach the usurper. But the sight of Kull, identical with the man upon the dais, held them in their tracks, their minds stunned for an instant, and that was long enough. He upon the dais snatched for his sword, but even as his fingers closed upon the hilt, Kull's sword stood out behind his shoulders and the thing that men had thought the king pitched forward from the dais to lie silent upon the floor.

"Hold!" Kull's lifted hand and kingly voice stopped the rush that had started, and while they stood astounded he pointed to the thing which lay before them-whose face was fading into that of a snake. They recoiled, and from one door came Brule and from another came Ka-nu.

These grasped the king's bloody hand and Ka-nu spoke: "Men of Valusia, you have seen with your own eyes. This is the true Kull, the mightiest king to whom Valusia has ever bowed. The power of the Serpent is broken and ye be all true men. King Kull, have you commands?"

"Lift that carrion," said Kull, and men of the guard took up the thing.

"Now follow me," said the king, and he made his way to the Accursed Room. Brule, with a look of concern, offered the support of his arm but Kull shook him off.

The distance seemed endless to the bleeding king, but at last he stood at the door and laughed fiercely and grimly when he heard the horrified ejaculations of the councilors.

At his orders the guardsmen flung the corpse they carried beside the others, and motioning all from the room Kull stepped out last and closed the door.

A wave of dizziness left him shaken. The faces turned to him, pallid and wonderingly, swirled and mingled in a ghostly fog. He felt the blood from his wound trickling down his limbs and he knew that what he was to do, he must do quickly or not at all.

His sword rasped from its sheath.

"Brule, are you there?"

"Aye!" Brule's face looked at him through the mist, close to his shoulder, but Brule's voice sounded leagues and eons away.

"Remember our vow, Brule. And now, bid them stand back."

His left arm cleared a space as he flung up his sword. Then with all his waning power he drove it through the door into the jamb, driving the great sword to the hilt and sealing the room forever.

Legs braced wide, he swayed drunkenly, facing the horrified councilors. "Let this room be doubly accursed. And let those rotting skeletons lie there forever as a sign of the dying might of the Serpent. Here I swear that I shall hunt the serpent-men from land to land, from sea to sea, giving no rest until all be slain, that good triumph and the power of Hell be broken. This thing I swear-I-Kull-king-of-Valusia."

His knees buckled as the faces swayed and swirled. The councilors leaped forward, but ere they could reach him, Kull slumped to the floor, and lay still, face upward.

The councilors surged about the fallen king, chattering and shrieking. Ka-nu beat them back with his clenched fists, cursing savagely.

"Back, you fools! Would you stifle the little life that is yet in him? How, Brule, is he dead or will he live?" – to the warrior who bent above the prostrate Kull.

"Dead?" sneered Brule irritably. "Such a man as this is not so easily killed. Lack of sleep and loss of blood have weakened him-by Valka, he has a score of deep wounds, but none of them mortal. Yet have those gibbering fools bring the court women here at once."

Brule's eyes lighted with a fierce, proud light.

"Valka, Ka-nu, but here is such a man as I knew not existed in these degenerate days. He will be in the saddle in a few scant days and then may the serpentmen of the world beware of Kull of Valusia. Valka! but that will be a rare hunt! Ah, I see long years of prosperity for the world with such a king upon the throne of Valusia."

The Mirrors of Tuzun Thune

"A wild, weird clime that lieth sublime Out of Space, out of Time."

—Poe

THERE comes, even to kings, the time of great weariness. Then the gold of the throne is brass, the silk of the palace becomes drab. The gems in the diadem sparkle drearily like the ice of the white seas; the speech of men is as the empty rattle of a jester's bell and the feel comes of things unreal; even the sun is copper in the sky, and the breath of the green ocean is no longer fresh.

Kull sat upon the throne of Valusia and the hour of weariness was upon him. They moved before him in an endless, meaningless panorama: men, women, priests, events and shadows of events; things seen and things to be attained. But like shadows they came and went, leaving no trace upon his consciousness, save that of a great mental fatigue. Yet Kull was not tired. There was a longing in him for things beyond himself and beyond the Valusian court. An unrest stirred in him, and strange, luminous dreams roamed his soul. At his bidding there came to him Brule the Spearslayer, warrior of Pictland, from the islands beyond the West.

"Lord king, you are tired of the life of the court. Come with me upon my galley and let us roam the tides for a space."

"Nay." Kull rested his chin moodily upon his mighty hand. "I am weary beyond all these things. The cities hold no lure for me-and the borders are quiet. I hear no more the sea-songs I heard when I lay as a boy on the booming crags of Atlantis, and the night was alive with blazing stars. No more do the green woodlands beckon me as of old. There is a strangeness upon me and a longing beyond life's longings. Go!"

Brule went forth in a doubtful mood, leaving the king brooding upon his throne. Then to Kull stole a girl of the court and whispered:

"Great king, seek Tuzun Thune, the wizard. The secrets of life and death are his, and the stars in the sky the lands beneath the seas." Kull looked at the girl. Fine gold was her hair and her violet eyes were slanted strangely; she was beautiful, but her beauty meant little to Kull.

"Tuzun Thune," he repeated. "Who is he?"

"A wizard of the Elder Race. He lives here in Valusia, by the Lake of Visions in the House of a Thousand Mirrors. All things are known to him, lord king; he speaks with the dead and holds converse with the demons of the Lost Lands."

Kull arose.

"I will seek out this mummer; but no word of my going, do you hear?"

"I am your slave, my lord." And she sank to her knees meekly, but the smile of her scarlet mouth was cunning behind Kull's back and the gleam of her narrow eyes was crafty.

Kull came to the house of Tuzun Thune, beside the Lake of Visions. Wide and blue stretched the waters of the lake, and many a fine palace rose upon its banks; many swan-winged pleasure boats drifted lazily upon its hazy surface and evermore there came the sound of soft music.

Tall and spacious, but unpretentious, rose the House of a Thousand Mirrors. The great doors stood open, and Kull ascended the broad stair and entered, unannounced. There in a great chamber, whose walls were of mirrors, he came upon Tuzun Thune, the wizard. The man was ancient as the hills of Zalgara; like wrinkled leather was his skin, but his cold gray eyes were like sparks of sword steel.

"Kull of Valusia, my house is yours," said he, bowing with old-time courtliness and motioning Kull to a throne-like chair.

"You are a wizard, I have heard," said Kull bluntly, resting his chin upon his hand and fixing his somber eyes upon the man's face. "Can you do wonders?"

The wizard stretched forth his hand; his fingers opened and closed like a bird's claws.

"Is that not a wonder-that this blind flesh obeys the thoughts of my mind? I walk, I breathe, I speak – are they not all wonders?"

Kull meditated awhile, then spoke. "Can you summon up demons?"

"Aye. I can summon up a demon more savage than any in ghost land-by smiting you in the face."

Kull started, then nodded. "But the dead, can you talk to the dead?"

"I talk with the dead always-as I am talking now. Death begins with birth, and each man begins to die when he is born; even now you are dead, King Kull, because you were born."

"But you, you are older than men become; do wizards never die?"

"Men die when their times come. No later, no sooner. Mine has not come."

Kull turned these answers over in his mind.

"Then it would seem that the greatest wizard of Valusia is no more than an ordinary man, and I have been duped in coming here."

Tuzun Thune shook his head. "Men are but men, and the greatest men are they who soonest learn the simpler things. Nay, look into my mirrors, Kull."

The ceiling was a great many mirrors, and the walls were mirrors, perfectly joined, yet many mirrors of many sizes and shapes.

"Mirrors are the world, Kull," droned the wizard. "Gaze into my mirrors and be wise."

Kull chose one at random and looked into it intently. The mirrors upon the opposite wall were reflected there, reflecting others, so that he seemed to be gazing down a long, luminous corridor, formed by mirror behind mirror; and far down this corridor moved a tiny figure. Kull looked long ere he saw that the figure was the reflection of himself. He gazed and a queer feeling of pettiness came over him; it seemed that that tiny figure was the true Kull, representing the real proportions of himself. So he moved away and stood before another.

"Look closely, Kull. That is the mirror of the past," he heard the wizard say.

Gray fogs obscured the vision, great billows of mist, ever heaving and changing like the ghost of a great river; through these fogs Kull caught swift fleeting visions of horror and strangeness; beasts and men moved there and shapes neither men nor beasts; great exotic blossoms glowed through the grayness; tall tropic trees towered high over reeking swamps, where reptilian monsters wallowed, and bellowed; the sky was ghastly with flying dragons, and the restless seas rocked and roared and beat endlessly along the muddy beaches. Man was not, yet man was the dream of the gods, and strange were the nightmare forms that glided through the noisome jungles. Battle and onslaught were there, and frightful love. Death was there, for Life and Death go hand in hand. Across the slimy beaches of the world sounded the bellowing of the monsters, and incredible shapes loomed through the streaming curtain of the incessant rain. "This is of the future." Kull looked in silence. "See you-what?"

"A strange world," said Kull heavily. "The Seven Empires are crumbled to dust and are forgotten. The restless green waves roar for many a fathom above the eternal hills of Atlantis; the mountains of Lemuria of the West are the islands of an unknown sea. Strange savages roam the elder lands and new lands flung strangely from the deeps, defiling the elder shrines. Valusia is vanished and all the nations of today; they of tomorrow are strangers. They know us not."

"Time strides onward," said Tuzun Thune calmly. "We live today; what care we for tomorrow-or yesterday? The Wheel turns and nations rise and fall; the world changes, and times return to savagery to rise again through the long age. Ere Atlantis was, Valusia was, and ere Valusia was, the Elder Nations were. Aye, we, too, trampled the shoulders of lost tribes in our advance. You, who have come from the green sea hills of Atlantis to seize the ancient crown of Valusia, you think my tribe is old, we who held these lands ere the Valusians came out of the East, in the days before there were men in the sea lands. But men were here when the Elder Tribes rode out of the waste lands, and men before men, tribe before tribe. The nations pass and are forgotten, for that is the destiny of man."

"Yes," said Kull. "Yet is it not a pity that the beauty and glory of men should fade like smoke on a summer sea?"

"For what reason, since that is their destiny? I brood not over the lost glories of my race, nor do I labor for races to come. Live now, Kull, live now. The dead are dead; the unborn are not. What matters men's forgetfulness of you when you have forgotten yourself in the silent worlds of death? Gaze in my mirrors and be wise."

Kull chose another mirror and gazed into it.

"That is the mirror of deepest magic; what see ye, Kull?"

"Naught but myself."

"Look closely, Kull; is it in truth you?"

Kull stared into the great mirror, and the image that was his reflection returned his gaze.

"I come before this mirror," mused Kull, chin on fist, "and I bring this man to life. That is beyond my understanding, since first I saw him in the still waters of the lakes of Atlantis, till I saw him again in the gold-rimmed mirrors of Valusia. He is I, a shadow of myself, part of myself-I can bring him into being or slay him at my will; yet–" He halted, strange thoughts whispering through the vast dim recesses of his mind like shadowy bats flying through a great cavern–"yet where is he when I stand not in front of a mirror? May it be in man's power thus lightly to form and destroy a shadow of life and existence? How do I know that when I step back from the mirror he vanishes into the void of Naught?"

"Nay, by Valka, am I the man or is he? Which of us is the ghost of the other? Mayhap these mirrors are but windows through which we look into another world. Does he think the same of me? Am I no more than a shadow, a reflection of himself-to him, as he to me? And if I am the ghost, what sort of a world lives upon the other side of this mirror? What armies ride there and what kings rule? This world is all I know. Knowing naught of any other, how can I judge? Surely there are green hills there and booming seas and wide plains where men ride to battle. Tell me, wizard who is wiser than most men, tell me are there worlds beyond our worlds?"

"A man has eyes, let him see," answered the wizard. "Who would see must first believe."

The hours drifted by, and Kull still sat before the mirrors of Tuzun Thune, gazing into that which depicted himself. Sometimes it seemed that he gazed upon hard shallowness; at other times gigantic depths seemed to loom before him. Like the surface of the sea was the mirror of Tuzun Thune; hard as the sea in the sun's slanting beams, in the darkness of the stars, when no eye can pierce her deeps; vast and mystic as the sea when the sun smites her in such way that the watcher's breath is caught at the glimpse of tremendous abysses. So was the mirror in which Kull gazed.

At last the king rose with a sigh and took his departure still wondering. And Kull came again to the House of a Thousand Mirrors; day after day he came and sat for hours before the mirror. The eyes looked out at him, identical with his; yet Kull seemed to sense a difference-a reality that was not of him. Hour upon hour he would stare with strange intensity into the mirror; hour after hour the image gave back his gaze.

The business of the palace and of the council went neglected. The people murmured; Kull's stallion stamped restlessly in his stable, and Kull's warriors diced and argued aimlessly with one another. Kull heeded not. At times he seemed on the point of discovering some vast, unthinkable secret. He no longer thought of the image in the mirror as a shadow of himself; the thing, to him, was an entity, similar in outer appearance, yet basically as far from Kull himself as the poles are far apart. The image, it seemed to Kull, had an individuality apart from Kull's, he was no more dependent on Kull than Kull was dependent on him. And day by day Kull doubted in which world he really lived; was he the shadow, summoned at will by the other? Did he instead of the other live in a world of delusion, the shadow of the real world?

Kull began to wish that he might enter the personality beyond the mirror for a space, to see what might be seen; yet should he manage to go beyond that door could he ever return? Would he find a world identical with the one in which he moved? A world, of which his was but a ghostly reflection? Which was reality and which illusion?

At times Kull halted to wonder how such thoughts and dreams had come to enter his mind, and at times he wondered if they came of his own volition or-here his thoughts would become mazed. His meditations were his own; no man ruled his thoughts, and he would summon them at his pleasure; yet could he? Were they not as bats, coming and going, not at his pleasure but at the bidding or ruling of-of whom? The gods? The Women who wove the webs of Fate? Kull could come to no conclusion, for at each mental step he became more and more bewildered in a hazy fog of illusory assertions and refutations. This much he knew: that strange visions entered his mind, like flying unbidden from the whispering void of non-existence; never had he thought these thoughts, but now they ruled his mind, sleeping and waking, so that he seemed to walk in a daze at times; and his sleep was fraught with strange, monstrous dreams.

"Tell me, wizard," he said, sitting before the mirror, eyes fixed intently upon his image, "how can I pass yon door? For of a truth, I am not sure that that is the real world and this the shadow; at least, that which I see must exist in some form."

"See and believe," droned the wizard. "Man must believe to accomplish. Form is shadow, substance is illusion, materiality is dream; man is because he believes he is; what is man but a dream of the gods? Yet man can be that which he wishes to be; form and substance, they are but shadows. The mind, the ego, the essence of the god-dream-that is real, that is immortal. See and believe, if you would accomplish, Kull."

The king did not fully understand; he never fully understood the enigmatical utterances of the wizard; yet they struck somewhere in his being a dim responsive chord. So day after day he sat before the mirrors of Tuzun Thune. Ever the wizard lurked behind him like a shadow.

Then came a day when Kull seemed to catch glimpses of strange lands; there flitted across his consciousness dim thoughts and recognitions. Day by day he had seemed to lose touch with the world; all things had seemed each succeeding day more ghostly and unreal; only the man in the mirror seemed like reality. Now Kull seemed to be close to the doors of some mightier worlds; giant vistas gleamed fleetingly; the fogs of unreality thinned; "form is shadow, substance is illusion; they are but shadows" sounded as if from some far country of his consciousness. He remembered the wizard's words and it seemed to him that now he almost understood-form and substance, could not he change himself at will, if he knew the master key that opened this door? What worlds within what worlds awaited the bold explorer?

The man in the mirror seemed smiling at him closer, closer-a fog enwrapped all and the reflection dimmed suddenly-Kull knew a sensation of fading, of change, of merging. . . .

"Kull!" the yell split the silence into a million vibratory fragments!

Mountains crashed and worlds tottered as Kull, hurled back by the frantic shout, made a superhuman effort, how or why he did not know.

A crash, and Kull stood in the room of Tuzun Thune before a shattered mirror, mazed and half blind with bewilderment. There before him lay the body of Tuzun Thune, whose time had come at last, and above him stood Brule the Spear-slayer, sword dripping red and eyes wide with a kind of horror.

"Valka!" swore the warrior. "Kull, it was time I came!"

"Aye, yet what happened?" The king groped for words.

"Ask this traitress," answered the Spear-slayer, indicating a girl who crouched in terror before the king; Kull saw that it was she who first sent him to Tuzun Thune. "As I came in I saw you fading into yon mirror as smoke fades into the sky, by Valka! Had I not seen I would not have believed-you had almost vanished when my shout brought you back."

"Aye," muttered Kull, "I had almost gone beyond the door that time."

"This fiend wrought most craftily," said Brule. "KULL, do you not now see how he spun and flung over you a web of magic? Kaanuub of Blaal plotted with this wizard to do away with you, and this wench, a girl of the Elder Race, put the thought in your mind so that you would come here. Ka-na of the council learned of the plot today; I know not what you saw in that mirror, but with it Tuzun Thune enthralled your soul and almost by his witchery he changed your body to mist–"

"Aye." Kull was still mazed. "But being a wizard, having knowledge of all the ages and despising gold, glory, and position, what could Kaanuub offer Tuzun Thune that would make of him a foul traitor?"

"Gold, power, and position," grunted Brule. "The sooner you learn that men are men whether wizard, king, or thrall, the better you will rule, Kull. Now what of her?"

"Naught, Brule," as the girl whimpered and groveled at Kull's feet. "She was but a tool. Rise, child, and go your ways; none shall harm you."

Alone with Brule, Kull looked for the last time on the mirrors of Tuzun Thune.

"Mayhap he plotted and conjured, Brule; nay, I doubt you not, yet-was it his witchery that was changing me to thin mist, or had I stumbled on a secret? Had you not brought me back, had I faded in dissolution or had I found worlds beyond this?"

Brule stole a glance at the mirrors, and twitched his shoulders as if he shuddered. "Aye, Tuzun Thune stored the wisdom of all the hells here. Let us be gone, Kull, ere they bewitch me, too."

"Let us go, then," answered Kull, and side by side they went forth from the House of a Thousand Mirrors-where, mayhap, are prisoned the souls of men.

None look now in the mirrors of Tuzun Thune. The pleasure boats shun the shore where stands the wizard's house, and no one goes in the house or to the room where Tuzun Thune's dried and withered carcass lies before the mirrors of illusion. The place is shunned as a place accursed, and though it stands for a thousand years to come, no footsteps shall echo there. Yet Kull upon his throne meditates often upon the strange wisdom and untold secrets hidden there and wonders. . .

For there are worlds beyond worlds, as Kull knows, and whether the wizard bewitched him by words or by mesmerism, vistas did open to the kings gaze beyond that strange door, and Kull is less sure of reality since he gazed into the mirrors of Tuzun Thune.

Kings of the Night

Chapter 1

The Caesar lolled on his ivory throne–
His iron legions came
To break a king in a land unknown,
And a race without a name.

—The Song of Bran

THE DAGGER flashed downward. A sharp cry broke in a gasp. The form on the rough altar twitched convulsively and lay still. The jagged flint edge sawed at the crimsoned breast, and thin bony fingers, ghastly dyed, tore out the still-twitching heart. Under matted white brows, sharp eyes gleamed with a ferocious intensity.

Besides the slayer, four men stood about the crude pile of stones that formed the altar of the God of Shadows. One was of medium height, lithely built, scantily clad, whose black hair was confined by a narrow iron band in the center of which gleamed a single red jewel. Of the others, two were dark like the first. But where he was lithe, they were stocky and misshapen, with knotted limbs, and tangled hair falling over sloping brows. His face denoted intelligence and implacable will; theirs merely a beast-like ferocity. The fourth man had little in common with the rest. Nearly a head taller, though his hair was black as theirs, his skin was comparatively light and he was gray-eyed. He eyed the proceedings with little favor.

And, in truth, Cormac of Connacht was little at ease. The Druids of his own isle of Erin had strange dark rites of worship, but nothing like this. Dark trees shut in this grim scene, lit by a single torch. Through the branches moaned an eerie night-wind. Cormac was alone among men of a strange race and he had just seen the heart of a man ripped from his still pulsing body. Now the ancient priest, who looked scarcely human, was glaring at the throbbing thing. Cormac shuddered, glancing at him who wore the jewel. Did Bran Mak Morn, king of the Picts, believe that this white-bearded old butcher could foretell events by scanning a bleeding human heart? The dark eyes of the king were inscrutable. There were strange depths to the man that Cormac could not fathom, nor any other man.

"The portents are good!" exclaimed the priest wildly, speaking more to the two chieftains than to Bran. "Here from the pulsing heart of a captive Roman I read – defeat for the arms of Rome! Triumph for the sons of the heather!"

The two savages murmured beneath their breath, their fierce eyes smoldering.

"Go and prepare your clans for battle," said the king, and they lumbered away with the ape-like gait assumed by such stunted giants. Paying no more heed to the priest who was examining the ghastly ruin on the altar, Bran beckoned to Cormac. The Gael followed him with alacrity. Once out of that grim grove, under the starlight, he breathed more freely. They stood on an eminence, looking out over long swelling undulations of gently waving heather. Near at hand a few fires twinkled, their fewness giving scant evidence of the hordes of tribesmen who lay close by. Beyond these were more fires and beyond these still more, which last marked the camp of Cormac's own men, hard-riding, hard-fighting Gaels, who were of that band which was just beginning to get a foothold on the western coast of Caledonia – the nucleus of what was later to become the kingdom of Dalriada. To the left of these, other fires gleamed.

And far away to the south were more fires – mere pinpoints of light. But even at that distance the Pictish king and his Celtic ally could see that these fires were laid out in regular order.

"The fires of the legions," muttered Bran. "The fires that have lit a path around the world. The men who light those fires have trampled the races under their iron heels. And now – we of the heather have our backs at the wall. What will fall on the morrow?"

"Victory for us, says the priest," answered Cormac.

Bran made an impatient gesture. "Moonlight on the ocean. Wind in the fir tops. Do you think that I put faith in such mummery? Or that I enjoyed the butchery of a captive legionary? I must hearten my people; it was for Gron and Bocah that I let old Gonar read the portents. The warriors will fight better."

"And Gonar?"

Bran laughed. "Gonar is too old to believe – anything. He was high priest of the Shadows a score of years before I was born. He claims direct descent from that Gonar who was a wizard in the days of Brule the Spear-slayer who was the first of my line. No man knows how old he is – sometimes I think he is the original Gonar himself!"

"At least," said a mocking voice, and Cormac started as a dim shape appeared at his side, "at least I have learned that in order to keep the faith and trust of the people, a wise man must appear to be a fool. I know secrets that would blast even your brain, Bran, should I speak them. But in order that the people may believe in me, I must descend to such things as they think proper magic – and prance and yell and rattle snakeskins, and dabble about in human blood and chicken livers."

Cormac looked at the ancient with new interest. The semi-madness of his appearance had vanished. He was no longer the charlatan, the spell-mumbling shaman. The starlight lent him a dignity which seemed to increase his very height, so that he stood like a white-bearded patriarch.

"Bran, your doubt lies there." The lean arm pointed to the fourth ring of fires.

"Aye," the king nodded gloomily. "Cormac – you know as well as I. Tomorrow's battle hinges upon that circle of fires. With the chariots of the Britons and your own Western horsemen, our success would be certain, but – surely the devil himself is in the heart of every Northman! You know how I trapped that band – how they swore to fight for me against Rome! And now that their chief, Rognar, is dead, they swear that they will be led only by a king of their own race! Else they will break their vow and go over to the Romans. Without them we are doomed, for we can not change our former plan."

"Take heart, Bran," said Gonar. "Touch the jewel in your iron crown. Mayhap it will bring you aid."

Bran laughed bitterly. "Now you talk as the people think. I am no fool to twist with empty words. What of the gem? It is a strange one, truth, and has brought me luck ere now. But I need now no jewels, but the allegiance of three hundred fickle Northmen who are the only warriors among us who may stand the charge of the legions on foot."

"But the jewel, Bran, the jewel!" persisted Gonar.

"Well, the jewel!" cried Bran impatiently. "It is older than this world. It was old when Atlantis and Lemuria sank into the sea. It was given to Brule, the Spear-slayer, first of my line, by the Atlantean Kull, king of Valusia, in the days when the world was young. But shall that profit us now?"

"Who knows?" asked the wizard obliquely. "Time and space exist not. There was no past, and there shall be no future. NOW is all. All things that ever were, are, or ever will be, transpire *now*. Man is forever at the center of what we call time and space. I have gone into yesterday and tomorrow and both were as real as today – which is like the dreams of ghosts! But let me sleep and talk with Gonar. Mayhap he shall aid us."

"What means he?" asked Cormac, with a slight twitching of his shoulders, as the priest strode away in the shadows.

"He has ever said that the first Gonar comes to him in his dreams and talks with him," answered Bran. "I have seen him perform deeds that seemed beyond human ken. I know not. I am but an unknown king with an iron crown, trying to lift a race of savages out of the slime into which they have sunk. Let us look to the camps."

As they walked Cormac wondered. By what strange freak of fate had such a man risen among this race of savages, survivors of a darker, grimmer age? Surely he was an atavism, an original type of the days when the Picts ruled all Europe, before their primitive empire fell before the bronze swords of the Gauls. Cormac knew how Bran, rising by his own efforts from the negligent position of the son of a Wolf clan chief, had to an extent united the tribes of the heather and now claimed kingship over all Caledon. But his rule was loose and much remained before the Pictish clans would forget their feuds and present a solid front to foreign foes. On the battle of the morrow, the first pitched battle between the Picts under their king and the Romans, hinged the future of the rising Pictish kingdom.

Bran and his ally walked through the Pictish camp where the swart warriors lay sprawled about their small fires, sleeping or gnawing half-cooked food. Cormac was impressed by their silence. A thousand men camped here, yet the only sounds were occasional low guttural intonations. The silence of the Stone Age rested in the souls of these men.

They were all short – most of them crooked of limb. Giant dwarfs; Bran Mak Morn was a tall man among them. Only the older men were bearded and they scantily, but their black hair fell about their eyes so that they peered fiercely from under the tangle. They were barefoot and clad scantily in wolfskins. Their arms consisted in short barbed swords of iron, heavy black bows, arrows tipped with flint, iron and copper, and stone-headed mallets. Defensive armor they had none, save for a crude shield of hide-covered wood; many had worked bits of metal into their tangled manes as a slight protection against sword-cuts. Some few, sons of long lines of chiefs, were smooth-limbed and lithe like Bran, but in the eyes of all gleamed the unquenchable savagery of the primeval.

These men are fully savages, thought Cormac, worse than the Gauls, Britons and Germans. Can the old legends be true – that they reigned in a day when strange cities rose where now the sea rolls? And that they survived the flood that washed those gleaming empires under, sinking again into that savagery from which they once had risen?

Close to the encampment of the tribesmen were the fires of a group of Britons – members of fierce tribes who lived south of the Roman Wall but who dwelt in the hills and forests to the west and defied the power of Rome. Powerfully built men they were, with blazing blue eyes and shocks of tousled yellow hair, such men as had thronged the Ceanntish beaches when Caesar brought the Eagles into the Isles. These men, like the Picts, wore no armor, and were clad scantily in coarse-worked cloth and deerskin sandals. They bore small round bucklers of hard wood, braced with bronze, to be worn on the left arm, and long heavy bronze swords with blunt points. Some had bows, though the Britons were indifferent archers. Their bows were shorter than the Picts' and effective only at close range. But ranged close by their fires were the weapons that had made the name Briton a word of terror to Pict, Roman and Norse raider alike. Within the circle of firelight stood fifty bronze chariots with long cruel blades curving out from the sides. One of these blades could dismember half a dozen men at once. Tethered close by under the vigilant eyes of their guards grazed the chariot horses – big, rangy steeds, swift and powerful.

"Would that we had more of them!" mused Bran. "With a thousand chariots and my bowmen I could drive the legions into the sea."

"The free British tribes must eventually fall before Rome," said Cormac. "It would seem they would rush to join you in your war."

Bran made a helpless gesture. "The fickleness of the Celt. They can not forget old feuds. Our ancient men have told us how they would not even unite against Caesar when the Romans first came. They will not make head against a common foe together. These men came to me because of some dispute with their chief, but I can not depend on them when they are not actually fighting."

Cormac nodded. "I know; Caesar conquered Gaul by playing one tribe against another. My own people shift and change with the waxing and waning of the tides. But of all Celts, the Cymry are the most changeable, the least stable. Not many centuries ago my own Gaelic ancestors wrested Erin from the Cymric Danaans, because though they outnumbered us, they opposed us as separate tribes, rather than as a nation."

"And so these Cymric Britons face Rome," said Bran. "These will aid us on the morrow. Further I can not say. But how shall I expect loyalty from alien tribes, who am not sure of my own people? Thousands lurk in the hills, holding aloof. I am king in name only. Let me win tomorrow and they will flock to my standard; if I lose, they will scatter like birds before a cold wind."

A chorus of rough welcome greeted the two leaders as they entered the camp of Cormac's Gaels. Five hundred in number they were, tall rangy men, black-haired and gray-eyed mainly, with the bearing of men who lived by war alone. While there was nothing like close discipline among them, there was an air of more system and practical order than existed in the lines of the Picts and Britons. These men were of the last Celtic race to invade the Isles and their barbaric civilization was of much higher order than that of their Cymric kin. The ancestors of the Gaels had learned the arts of war on the vast plains of Scythia and at the courts of the Pharaohs where they had fought as mercenaries of Egypt, and much of what they learned they brought into Ireland with them. Excelling in metal work, they were armed, not with clumsy bronze swords, but with high-grade weapons of iron.

They were clad in well-woven kilts and leathern sandals. Each wore a light shirt of chain mail and a vizorless helmet, but this was all of their defensive armor. Celts, Gaelic or Brythonic, were prone to judge a man's valor by the amount of armor he wore. The Britons who faced Caesar deemed the Romans cowards because they cased themselves in metal, and many centuries later the Irish clans thought the same of the mail-clad Norman knights of Strongbow.

Cormac's warriors were horsemen. They neither knew nor esteemed the use of the bow. They bore the inevitable round, metal-braced buckler, dirks, long straight swords and light single-handed axes. Their tethered horses grazed not far away – big-boned animals, not so ponderous as those raised by the Britons, but swifter.

Bran's eyes lighted as the two strode through the camp. "These men are keen-beaked birds of war! See how they whet their axes and jest of the morrow! Would that the raiders in yon camp were as staunch as your men, Cormac! Then would I greet the legions with a laugh when they come up from the south tomorrow."

They were entering the circle of the Northmen fires. Three hundred men sat about gambling, whetting their weapons and drinking deep of the heather ale furnished them by their Pictish allies. These gazed upon Bran and Cormac with no great friendliness. It was striking to note the difference between them and the Picts and Celts – the difference in their cold eyes, their strong moody faces, their very bearing. Here was ferocity, and savagery, but not of the wild, upbursting fury of the Celt. Here was fierceness backed by grim determination and stolid stubbornness. The charge of the British clans was terrible, overwhelming. But they had no patience; let them be balked of immediate victory and they were likely to lose heart and scatter or fall to bickering among themselves. There was the patience of the cold blue North in these seafarers – a lasting determination that would keep them steadfast to the bitter end, once their face was set toward a definite goal.

As to personal stature, they were giants; massive yet rangy. That they did not share the ideas of the Celts regarding armor was shown by the fact that they were clad in heavy scale mail shirts that reached below mid-thigh, heavy horned helmets and hardened hide leggings, reinforced, as were their shoes, with plates of iron. Their shields were huge oval affairs of hard wood, hide and brass. As to weapons, they had long iron-headed spears, heavy iron axes, and daggers. Some had long wide-bladed swords.

Cormac scarcely felt at ease with the cold magnetic eyes of these flaxen-haired men fixed upon him. He and they were hereditary foes, even though they did chance to be fighting on the same side at present – but were they?

A man came forward, a tall gaunt warrior on whose scarred, wolfish face the flickering firelight reflected deep shadows. With his wolfskin mantle flung carelessly about his wide shoulders, and the great horns on his helmet adding to his height, he stood there in the swaying shadows, like some half-human thing, a brooding shape of the dark barbarism that was soon to engulf the world.

"Well, Wulfhere," said the Pictish king, "you have drunk the mead of council and have spoken about the fires – what is your decision?"

The Northman's eyes flashed in the gloom. "Give us a king of our own race to follow if you wish us to fight for you."

Bran flung out his hands. "Ask me to drag down the stars to gem your helmets! Will not your comrades follow you?"

"Not against the legions," answered Wulfhere sullenly. "A king led us on the Viking path – a king must lead us against the Romans. And Rognar is dead."

"I am a king," said Bran. "Will you fight for me if I stand at the tip of your fight wedge?"

"A king of our own race," said Wulfhere doggedly. "We are all picked men of the North. We fight for none but a king, and a king must lead us – against the legions."

Cormac sensed a subtle threat in this repeated phrase.

"Here is a prince of Erin," said Bran. "Will you fight for the Westerner?"

"We fight under no Celt, West or East," growled the Viking, and a low rumble of approval rose from the onlookers. "It is enough to fight by their side."

The hot Gaelic blood rose in Cormac's brain and he pushed past Bran, his hand on his sword. "How mean you that, pirate?"

Before Wulfhere could reply Bran interposed: "Have done! Will you fools throw away the battle before it is fought, by your madness? What of your oath, Wulfhere?"

"We swore it under Rognar; when he died from a Roman arrow we were absolved of it. We will follow only a king – against the legions."

"But your comrades will follow you – against the heather people!" snapped Bran.

"Aye," the Northman's eyes met his brazenly. "Send us a king or we join the Romans tomorrow."

Bran snarled. In his rage he dominated the scene, dwarfing the huge men who towered over him.

"Traitors! Liars! I hold your lives in my hand! Aye, draw your swords if you will – Cormac, keep your blade in its sheath. These wolves will not bite a king! Wulfhere – I spared your lives when I could have taken them.

"You came to raid the countries of the South, sweeping down from the northern sea in your galleys. You ravaged the coasts and the smoke of burning villages hung like a cloud over the shores of Caledon. I trapped you all when you were pillaging and burning – with the blood of my people on your hands. I burned your long ships and ambushed you when you followed. With thrice your number of bowmen who burned for your lives hidden in the heathered hills about you, I spared you when we could have shot you down like trapped wolves. Because I spared you, you swore to come and fight for me."

"And shall we die because the Picts fight Rome?" rumbled a bearded raider.

"Your lives are forfeit to me; you came to ravage the South. I did not promise to send you all back to your homes in the North unharmed and loaded with loot. Your vow was to fight one battle against Rome under my standard. Then I will aid your survivors to build ships and you may go where you will, with a goodly share of the plunder we take from the legions. Rognar had kept his oath. But Rognar died in a skirmish with Roman scouts and now you, Wulfhere the Dissension-breeder, you stir up your comrades to dishonor themselves by that which a Northman hates – the breaking of the sworn word."

"We break no oath," snarled the Viking, and the king sensed the basic Germanic stubbornness, far harder to combat than the fickleness of the fiery Celts. "Give us a king, neither Pict, Gael nor Briton, and we will die for you. If not – then we will fight tomorrow for the greatest of all kings – the emperor of Rome!"

For a moment Cormac thought that the Pictish king, in his black rage, would draw and strike the Northman dead. The concentrated fury that blazed in Bran's dark eyes caused Wulfhere to recoil and drop a hand to his belt.

"Fool!" said Mak Morn in a low voice that vibrated with passion. "I could sweep you from the earth before the Romans are near enough to hear your death howls. Choose – fight for me on the morrow – or die tonight under a black cloud of arrows, a red storm of swords, a dark wave of chariots!"

At the mention of the chariots, the only arm of war that had ever broken the Norse shield-wall, Wulfhere changed expression, but he held his ground.

"War be it," he said doggedly. "Or a king to lead us!"

The Northmen responded with a short deep roar and a clash of swords on shields. Bran, eyes blazing, was about to speak again when a white shape glided silently into the ring of firelight.

"Soft words, soft words," said old Gonar tranquilly. "King, say no more. Wulfhere, you and your fellows will fight for us if you have a king to lead you?"

"We have sworn."

"Then be at ease," quoth the wizard; "for ere battle joins on the morrow I will send you such a king as no man on earth has followed for a hundred thousand years! A king neither Pict, Gael nor Briton, but one to whom the emperor of Rome is as but a village headman!"

While they stood undecided, Gonar took the arms of Cormac and Bran. "Come. And you, Northmen, remember your vow, and my promise which I have never broken. Sleep now, nor think to steal away in the darkness to the Roman camp, for if you escaped our shafts you would not escape either my curse or the suspicions of the legionaries."

So the three walked away and Cormac, looking back, saw Wulfhere standing by the fire, fingering his golden beard, with a look of puzzled anger on his lean evil face.

The three walked silently through the waving heather under the faraway stars while the weird night wind whispered ghostly secrets about them.

"Ages ago," said the wizard suddenly, "in the days when the world was young, great lands rose where now the ocean roars. On these lands thronged mighty nations and kingdoms. Greatest of all these was Valusia – Land of Enchantment. Rome is as a village compared to the splendor of the cities of Valusia. And the greatest king was Kull, who came from the land of Atlantis to wrest the crown of Valusia from a degenerate dynasty. The Picts who dwelt in the isles which now form the mountain peaks of a strange land upon the Western Ocean, were allies of Valusia, and the greatest of all the Pictish war-chiefs was Brule the Spear-slayer, first of the line men call Mak Morn.

"Kull gave to Brule the jewel which you now wear in your iron crown, oh king, after a strange battle in a dim land, and down the long ages it has come to us, ever a sign of the Mak Morn, a symbol of former greatness. When at last the sea rose and swallowed Valusia, Atlantis and Lemuria, only the Picts survived and they were scattered and few. Yet they began again the slow climb upward, and though many of the arts of civilization were lost in the great flood, yet they progressed. The art of metalworking was lost, so they excelled in the working of flint. And they ruled all the new lands flung up by the sea and now called Europe, until down from the north came younger tribes who had scarce risen from the ape when Valusia reigned in her glory, and who, dwelling in the icy lands about the Pole, knew naught of the lost splendor of the Seven Empires and little of the flood that had swept away half a world.

"And still they have come – Aryans, Celts, Germans, swarming down from the great cradle of their race which lies near the Pole. So again was the growth of the Pictish nation checked and the race hurled into savagery. Erased from the earth, on the fringe of the world with our backs to the wall we fight. Here in Caledon is the last stand of a once mighty race. And we change. Our people have mixed with the savages of an elder age which we drove into the North when we came into the Isles, and now, save for their chieftains, such as thou, Bran, a Pict is strange and abhorrent to look upon."

"True, true," said the king impatiently, "but what has that to do–"

"Kull, king of Valusia," said the wizard imperturbably, "was a barbarian in his age as thou art in thine, though he ruled a mighty empire by the weight of his sword. Gonar, friend of Brule, your first ancestor, has been dead a hundred thousand years as we reckon time. Yet I talked with him a scant hour agone."

"You talked with his ghost–"

"Or he with mine? Did I go back a hundred thousand years, or did he come forward? If he came to me out of the past, it is not I who talked with a dead man, but he who talked with a man unborn. Past, present and future are one to a wise man. I talked to Gonar while he was alive; likewise was I alive. In a timeless, spaceless land we met and he told me many things."

The land was growing light with the birth of dawn. The heather waved and bent in long rows before the dawn wind as bowing in worship of the rising sun.

"The jewel in your crown is a magnet that draws down the eons," said Gonar. "The sun is rising – and who comes out of the sunrise?"

Cormac and the king started. The sun was just lifting a red orb above the eastern hills. And full in the glow, etched boldly against the golden rim, a man suddenly appeared. They had not seen him come. Against the golden birth of day he loomed colossal; a gigantic god from the dawn of creation. Now as he strode toward them the waking hosts saw him and sent up a sudden shout of wonder.

"Who – or what is it?" exclaimed Bran.

"Let us go to meet him, Bran," answered the wizard. "He is the king Gonar has sent to save the people of Brule."

Chapter 2

"I have reached these lands but newly
From an ultimate dim Thule;
From a wild weird clime that lieth sublime
Out of Space – out of Time."

—Poe.

The army fell silent as Bran, Cormac and Gonar went toward the stranger who approached in long swinging strides. As they neared him the illusion of monstrous size vanished, but they saw he was a man of great stature. At first Cormac thought him to be a Northman but a second glance told him that nowhere before had he seen such a man. He was built much like the Vikings, at once massive and lithe – tigerish. But his features were not as theirs, and his square-cut, lion-like mane of hair was as black as Bran's own. Under heavy brows glittered eyes gray as steel and cold as ice. His bronzed face, strong and inscrutable, was clean-shaven, and the broad forehead betokened a high intelligence, just as the firm jaw and thin lips showed willpower and courage. But more than all, the bearing of him, the unconscious lion-like stateliness, marked him as a natural king, a ruler of men.

Sandals of curious make were on his feet and he wore a pliant coat of strangely meshed mail which came almost to his knees. A broad belt with a great golden buckle encircled his waist, supporting a long straight sword in a heavy leather scabbard. His hair was confined by a wide, heavy golden band about his head.

Such was the man who paused before the silent group. He seemed slightly puzzled, slightly amused. Recognition flickered in his eyes. He spoke in a strange archaic Pictish which Cormac scarcely understood. His voice was deep and resonant.

"Ha, Brule, Gonar did not tell me I would dream of you!"

For the first time in his life Cormac saw the Pictish king completely thrown off his balance. He gaped, speechless. The stranger continued:

"And wearing the gem I gave you, in a circlet on your head! Last night you wore it in a ring on your finger."

"Last night?" gasped Bran.

"Last night or a hundred thousand years ago – all one!" murmured Gonar in evident enjoyment of the situation.

"I am not Brule," said Bran. "Are you mad to thus speak of a man dead a hundred thousand years? He was first of my line."

The stranger laughed unexpectedly. "Well, now I know I am dreaming! This will be a tale to tell Brule when I waken on the morrow! That I went into the future and saw men claiming descent from the Spear-slayer who is, as yet, not even married. No, you are not Brule, I see now, though you have his eyes and his bearing. But he is taller and broader in the shoulders. Yet you have his jewel – oh, well – anything can happen in a dream, so I will not quarrel with you. For a time I thought I had been transported to some other land in my sleep, and was in reality awake in a strange country, for this is the clearest dream I ever dreamed. Who are you?"

"I am Bran Mak Morn, king of the Caledonian Picts. And this ancient is Gonar, a wizard, of the line of Gonar. And this warrior is Cormac na Connacht, a prince of the isle of Erin."

The stranger slowly shook his lion-like head. "These words sound strangely to me, save Gonar – and that one is not Gonar, though he too is old. What land is this?"

"Caledon, or Alba, as the Gaels call it."

"And who are those squat ape-like warriors who watch us yonder, all agape?"

"They are the Picts who own my rule."

"How strangely distorted folk are in dreams!" muttered the stranger. "And who are those shock-headed men about the chariots?"

"They are Britons – Cymry from south of the Wall."

"What Wall?"

"The Wall built by Rome to keep the people of the heather out of Britain."

"Britain?" the tone was curious. "I never heard of that land – and what is Rome?"

"What!" cried Bran. "You never heard of Rome, the empire that rules the world?"

"No empire rules the world," answered the other haughtily. "The mightiest kingdom on Earth is that wherein I reign."

"And who are you?"

"Kull of Atlantis, king of Valusia!"

Cormac felt a coldness trickle down his spine. The cold gray eyes were unswerving – but this was incredible – monstrous – unnatural.

"Valusia!" cried Bran. "Why, man, the sea waves have rolled above the spires of Valusia for untold centuries!"

Kull laughed outright. "What a mad nightmare this is! When Gonar put on me the spell of deep sleep last night – or this night! – in the secret room of the inner palace, he told me I would dream strange things, but this is more fantastic than I reckoned. And the strangest thing is, I know I am dreaming!"

Gonar interposed as Bran would have spoken. "Question not the acts of the gods," muttered the wizard. "You are king because in the past you have seen and seized opportunities. The gods or the first Gonar have sent you this man. Let me deal with him."

Bran nodded, and while the silent army gaped in speechless wonder, just within earshot, Gonar spoke: "Oh great king, you dream, but is not all life a dream? How reckon you but that your former life is but a dream from which you have just awakened? Now we dream-folk have our wars and our peace, and just now a great host comes up from the south to destroy the people of Brule. Will you aid us?"

Kull grinned with pure zest. "Aye! I have fought battles in dreams ere now, have slain and been slain and was amazed when I woke from my visions. And at times, as now, dreaming I have known I dreamed. See, I pinch myself and feel it, but I know I dream for I have felt the pain of fierce wounds, in dreams. Yes, people of my dream, I will fight for you against the other dream-folk. Where are they?"

"And that you enjoy the dream more," said the wizard subtly, "forget that it is a dream and pretend that by the magic of the first Gonar, and the quality of the jewel you gave Brule, that now gleams on the crown of the Morni, you have in truth been transported forward into another, wilder age where the people of Brule fight for their life against a stronger foe."

For a moment the man who called himself king of Valusia seemed startled; a strange look of doubt, almost of fear, clouded his eyes. Then he laughed.

"Good! Lead on, wizard."

But now Bran took charge. He had recovered himself and was at ease. Whether he thought, like Cormac, that this was all a gigantic hoax arranged by Gonar, he showed no sign.

"King Kull, see you those men yonder who lean on their long-shafted axes as they gaze upon you?"

"The tall men with the golden hair and beards?"

"Aye – our success in the coming battle hinges on them. They swear to go over to the enemy if we give them not a king to lead them – their own having been slain. Will you lead them to battle?"

Kull's eyes glowed with appreciation. "They are men such as my own Red Slayers, my picked regiment. I will lead them."

"Come then."

The small group made their way down the slope, through throngs of warriors who pushed forward eagerly to get a better view of the stranger, then pressed back as he approached. An undercurrent of tense whispering ran through the horde.

The Northmen stood apart in a compact group. Their cold eyes took in Kull and he gave back their stares, taking in every detail of their appearance.

"Wulfhere," said Bran, "we have brought you a king. I hold you to your oath."

"Let him speak to us," said the Viking harshly.

"He can not speak your tongue," answered Bran, knowing that the Northmen knew nothing of the legends of his race. "He is a great king of the South–"

"He comes out of the past," broke in the wizard calmly. "He was the greatest of all kings, long ago."

"A dead man!" The Vikings moved uneasily and the rest of the horde pressed forward, drinking in every word.

But Wulfhere scowled: "Shall a ghost lead living men? You bring us a man you say is dead. We will not follow a corpse."

"Wulfhere," said Bran in still passion, "you are a liar and a traitor. You set us this task, thinking it impossible. You yearn to fight under the Eagles of Rome. We have brought you a king neither Pict, Gael nor Briton and you deny your vow!"

"Let him fight me, then!" howled Wulfhere in uncontrollable wrath, swinging his ax about his head in a glittering arc. "If your dead man overcomes me – then my people will follow you. If I overcome him, you shall let us depart in peace to the camp of the legions!"

"Good!" said the wizard. "Do you agree, wolves of the North?"

A fierce yell and a brandishing of swords was the answer. Bran turned to Kull, who had stood silent, understanding nothing of what was said. But the Atlantean's eyes gleamed. Cormac felt that those cold eyes had looked on too many such scenes not to understand something of what had passed.

"This warrior says you must fight him for the leadership," said Bran, and Kull, eyes glittering with growing battle-joy, nodded: "I guessed as much. Give us space."

"A shield and a helmet!" shouted Bran, but Kull shook his head.

"I need none," he growled. "Back and give us room to swing our steel!"

Men pressed back on each side, forming a solid ring about the two men, who now approached each other warily. Kull had drawn his sword and the great blade shimmered like a live thing in his hand. Wulfhere, scarred by a hundred savage fights, flung aside his wolfskin mantle and came in cautiously, fierce eyes peering over the top of his out-thrust shield, ax half-lifted in his right hand.

Suddenly when the warriors were still many feet apart Kull sprang. His attack brought a gasp from men used to deeds of prowess; for like a leaping tiger he shot through the air and his sword crashed on the quickly lifted shield. Sparks flew and Wulfhere's ax hacked in, but Kull was under its sweep and as it swished viciously above his head he thrust upward and sprang out again, cat-like. His motions had been too quick for the eye to follow. The upper edge of Wulfhere's shield showed a deep cut, and there was a long rent in his mail shirt where Kull's sword had barely missed the flesh beneath.

Cormac, trembling with the terrible thrill of the fight, wondered at this sword that could thus slice through scale-mail. And the blow that gashed the shield should have shattered the blade. Yet not a notch showed in the Valusian steel! Surely this blade was forged by another people in another age!

Now the two giants leaped again to the attack and like double strokes of lightning their weapons crashed. Wulfhere's shield fell from his arm in two pieces as the Atlantean's sword sheared clear through it, and Kull staggered as the Northman's ax, driven with all the force of his great body, descended on the golden circlet about his head. That blow should have sheared through the gold like butter to split the skull beneath, but the ax rebounded, showing a great notch in the edge. The next instant the Northman was overwhelmed by a whirlwind of steel – a storm of strokes delivered with such swiftness and power that he was borne back as on the crest of a wave, unable to launch an attack of his own. With all his tried skill he sought to parry the singing steel with his ax. But he could only avert his doom for a few seconds; could only for an instant turn the whistling blade that hewed off bits of his mail, so close fell the blows. One of the horns flew from his helmet; then the ax-head itself fell away, and the same blow that severed the handle, bit through the Viking's helmet into the scalp beneath. Wulfhere was dashed to his knees, a trickle of blood starting down his face.

Kull checked his second stroke, and tossing his sword to Cormac, faced the dazed Northman weaponless. The Atlantean's eyes were blazing with ferocious joy and he roared something in a strange tongue. Wulfhere gathered his legs under him and bounded up, snarling like a wolf, a dagger flashing into his hand. The watching horde gave tongue in a yell that ripped the skies as the two bodies clashed. Kull's clutching hand missed the Northman's wrist but the desperately lunging dagger snapped on the Atlantean's mail, and dropping the useless hilt, Wulfhere locked his arms about his foe in a bear-like grip that would have crushed the ribs of a lesser man. Kull grinned tigerishly and returned the grapple, and for a moment the two swayed on their feet. Slowly the black-haired warrior bent his foe backward until it seemed his spine would snap. With a howl that had nothing of the human in it, Wulfhere clawed frantically at Kull's face, trying to tear out his eyes, then turned his head and snapped his fang-like teeth into the Atlantean's arm. A yell went up as a trickle of blood started: "He bleeds! He bleeds! He is no ghost, after all, but a mortal man!"

Angered, Kull shifted his grip, shoving the frothing Wulfhere away from him, and smote him terrifically under the ear with his right hand. The Viking landed on his back a dozen feet away. Then, howling like a wild man, he leaped up with a stone in his hand and flung it. Only Kull's incredible quickness saved his face; as it was, the rough edge of the missile tore his cheek and inflamed him to madness. With a lion-like roar he bounded upon his foe, enveloped him in an irresistible blast of sheer fury, whirled him high above his head as if he were a child and cast him a dozen feet away. Wulfhere pitched on his head and lay still – broken and dead.

Dazed silence reigned for an instant; then from the Gaels went up a thundering roar, and the Britons and Picts took it up, howling like wolves, until the echoes of the shouts and the clangor of sword on shield reached the ears of the marching legionaries, miles to the south.

"Men of the gray North," shouted Bran, "will you hold by your oath *now?*"

The fierce souls of the Northmen were in their eyes as their spokesman answered. Primitive, superstitious, steeped in tribal lore of fighting gods and mythical heroes, they did not doubt that the black-haired fighting man was some supernatural being sent by the fierce gods of battle.

"Aye! Such a man as this we have never seen! Dead man, ghost or devil, we will follow him, whether the trail lead to Rome or Valhalla!"

Kull understood the meaning, if not the words. Taking his sword from Cormac with a word of thanks, he turned to the waiting Northmen and silently held the blade toward them high above his head, in both hands, before he returned it to its scabbard. Without understanding, they appreciated the action. Bloodstained and disheveled, he was an impressive picture of stately, magnificent barbarism.

"Come," said Bran, touching the Atlantean's arm; "a host is marching on us and we have much to do. There is scant time to arrange our forces before they will be upon us. Come to the top of yonder slope."

There the Pict pointed. They were looking down into a valley which ran north and south, widening from a narrow gorge in the north until it debouched upon a plain to the south. The whole valley was less than a mile in length.

"Up this valley will our foes come," said the Pict, "because they have wagons loaded with supplies and on all sides of this vale the ground is too rough for such travel. Here we plan an ambush."

"I would have thought you would have had your men lying in wait long before now," said Kull. "What of the scouts the enemy is sure to send out?"

"The savages I lead would never have waited in ambush so long," said Bran with a touch of bitterness. "I could not post them until I was sure of the Northmen. Even so I had not dared to post them ere now – even yet they may take panic from the drifting of a cloud or the blowing of a leaf, and scatter like birds before a cold wind. King Kull – the fate of the Pictish nation is at stake. I am called king of the

Picts, but my rule as yet is but a hollow mockery. The hills are full of wild clans who refuse to fight for me. Of the thousand bowmen now at my command, more than half are of my own clan.

"Some eighteen hundred Romans are marching against us. It is not a real invasion, but much hinges upon it. It is the beginning of an attempt to extend their boundaries. They plan to build a fortress a day's march to the north of this valley. If they do, they will build other forts, drawing bands of steel about the heart of the free people. If I win this battle and wipe out this army, I will win a double victory. Then the tribes will flock to me and the next invasion will meet a solid wall of resistance. If I lose, the clans will scatter, fleeing into the north until they can no longer flee, fighting as separate clans rather than as one strong nation.

"I have a thousand archers, five hundred horsemen, fifty chariots with their drivers and swordsmen – one hundred fifty men in all – and, thanks to you, three hundred heavily armed Northern pirates. How would you arrange your battle lines?"

"Well," said Kull, "I would have barricaded the north end of the valley – no! That would suggest a trap. But I would block it with a band of desperate men, like those you have given me to lead. Three hundred could hold the gorge for a time against any number. Then, when the enemy was engaged with these men to the narrow part of the valley, I would have my archers shoot down into them until their ranks are broken, from both sides of the vale. Then, having my horsemen concealed behind one ridge and my chariots behind the other, I would charge with both simultaneously and sweep the foe into a red ruin."

Bran's eyes glowed. "Exactly, king of Valusia. Such was my exact plan–"

"But what of the scouts?"

"My warriors are like panthers; they hide under the noses of the Romans. Those who ride into the valley will see only what we wish them to see. Those who ride over the ridge will not come back to report. An arrow is swift and silent.

"You see that the pivot of the whole thing depends on the men that hold the gorge. They must be men who can fight on foot and resist the charges of the heavy legionaries long enough for the trap to close. Outside these Northmen I had no such force of men. My naked warriors with their short swords could never stand such a charge for an instant. Nor is the armor of the Celts made for such work; moreover, they are not foot-fighters, and I need them elsewhere.

"So you see why I had such desperate need of the Northmen. Now will you stand in the gorge with them and hold back the Romans until I can spring the trap? Remember, most of you will die."

Kull smiled. "I have taken chances all my life, though Tu, chief councilor, would say my life belongs to Valusia and I have no right to so risk it–" His voice trailed off and a strange look flitted across his face. "By Valka," said he, laughing uncertainly, "sometimes I forget this is a dream! All seems so real. But it is – of course it is! Well, then, if I die I will but awaken as I have done in times past. Lead on, king of Caledon!"

Cormac, going to his warriors, wondered. Surely it was all a hoax; yet – he heard the arguments of the warriors all about him as they armed themselves and prepared to take their posts. The black-haired king was Neid himself, the Celtic war-god; he was an antediluvian king brought out of the past by Gonar; he was a mythical fighting man out of Valhalla. He was no man at all but a ghost! No, he was mortal, for he had bled. But the gods themselves bled, though they did not die. So the controversies raged. At least, thought Cormac, if it was all a hoax to inspire the warriors with the feeling of supernatural aid, it had succeeded. The belief that Kull was more than a mortal man had fired Celt, Pict and Viking alike into a sort of inspired madness. And Cormac asked himself – what did he himself believe? This man was surely one from some far land – yet in his every look and action there was a vague hint of a greater difference than mere distance of space – a hint of alien Time, of misty abysses and gigantic gulfs of eons lying between the black-haired stranger and the men with whom he walked and talked. Clouds of bewilderment mazed Cormac's brain and he laughed in whimsical self-mockery.

Chapter 3

"And the two wild peoples of the north
Stood fronting in the gloam,
And heard and knew each in his mind
A third great sound upon the wind,
The living walls that hedge mankind,
The walking walls of Rome."

—Chesterton.

The sun slanted westward. Silence lay like an invisible mist over the valley. Cormac gathered the reins in his hand

and glanced up at the ridges on both sides. The waving heather which grew rank on those steep slopes gave no evidence of the hundreds of savage warriors who lurked there. Here in the narrow gorge which widened gradually southward was the only sign of life. Between the steep walls three hundred Northmen were massed solidly in their wedge-shaped shield-wall, blocking the pass. At the tip, like the point of a spear, stood the man who called himself Kull, king of Valusia. He wore no helmet, only the great, strangely worked head-band of hard gold, but he bore on his left arm the great shield borne by the dead Rognar; and in his right hand he held the heavy iron mace wielded by the sea-king. The Vikings eyed him in wonder and savage admiration. They could not understand his language, or he theirs. But no further orders were necessary. At Bran's directions they had bunched themselves in the gorge, and their only order was – hold the pass!

Bran Mak Morn stood just in front of Kull. So they faced each other, he whose kingdom was yet unborn, and he whose kingdom had been lost in the mists of Time for unguessed ages. Kings of darkness, thought Cormac, nameless kings of the night, whose realms are gulfs and shadows.

The hand of the Pictish king went out. "King Kull, you are more than king – you are a man. Both of us may fall within the next hour – but if we both live, ask what you will of me."

Kull smiled, returning the firm grip. "You too are a man after my own heart, king of the shadows. Surely you are more than a figment of my sleeping imagination. Mayhap we will meet in waking life some day."

Bran shook his head in puzzlement, swung into the saddle and rode away, climbing the eastern slope and vanishing over the ridge. Cormac hesitated: "Strange man, are you in truth of flesh and blood, or are you a ghost?"

"When we dream, we are all flesh and blood – so long as we are dreaming," Kull answered. "This is the strangest nightmare I have ever known – but you, who will soon fade into sheer nothingness as I awaken, seem as real to me *now*, as Brule, or Kananu, or Tu, or Kelkor."

Cormac shook his head as Bran had done, and with a last salute, which Kull returned with barbaric stateliness, he turned and trotted away. At the top of the western ridge he paused. Away to the south a light cloud of dust rose and the head of the marching column was in sight. Already he believed he could feel the earth vibrate slightly to the measured tread of a thousand mailed feet beating in perfect unison. He dismounted, and one of his chieftains, Domnail, took his steed and led it down the slope away from the valley, where trees grew thickly. Only an occasional vague movement among them gave evidence of the five hundred men who stood there, each at his horse's head with a ready hand to check a chance nicker.

Oh, thought Cormac, *the gods themselves made this valley for Bran's ambush!* The floor of the valley was treeless and the inner slopes were bare save for the waist-high heather. But at the foot of each ridge on the side facing away from the vale, where the soil long washed from the rocky slopes had accumulated, there grew enough trees to hide five hundred horsemen or fifty chariots.

At the northern end of the valley stood Kull and his three hundred Vikings, in open view, flanked on each side by fifty Pictish bowmen. Hidden on the western side of the western ridge were the Gaels. Along the top of the slopes, concealed in the tall heather, lay a hundred Picts with their shafts on string. The rest of the Picts were hidden on the eastern slopes beyond which lay the Britons with their chariots in full readiness. Neither they nor the Gaels to the west could see what went on in the vale, but signals had been arranged.

Now the long column was entering the wide mouth of the valley and their scouts, light-armed men on swift horses, were spreading out between the slopes. They galloped almost within bowshot of the silent host that blocked the pass, then halted. Some whirled and raced back to the main force, while the others deployed and cantered up the slopes, seeking to see what lay beyond. This was the crucial moment. If they got any hint of the ambush, all was lost. Cormac, shrinking down into the heather, marveled at the ability of the Picts to efface themselves from view so completely. He saw a horseman pass within three feet of where he knew a bowman lay, yet the Roman saw nothing.

The scouts topped the ridges, gazed about; then most of them turned and trotted back down the slopes. Cormac wondered at their desultory manner of scouting. He had never fought Romans before, knew nothing of their arrogant self-confidence, of their incredible shrewdness in some ways, their incredible stupidity in others. These men were overconfident; a feeling radiating from their officers. It had been years since a force of Caledonians had stood before the legions. And most of these men were but newly come to

Britain; part of a legion which had been quartered in Egypt. They despised their foes and suspected nothing.

But stay – three riders on the opposite ridge had turned and vanished on the other side. And now one, sitting his steed at the crest of the western ridge, not a hundred yards from where Cormac lay, looked long and narrowly down into the mass of trees at the foot of the slope. Cormac saw suspicion grow on his brown, hawk-like face. He half turned as though to call to his comrades, then instead reined his steed down the slope, leaning forward in his saddle. Cormac's heart pounded. Each moment he expected to see the man wheel and gallop back to raise the alarm. He resisted a mad impulse to leap up and charge the Roman on foot. Surely the man could feel the tenseness in the air – the hundreds of fierce eyes upon him. Now he was halfway down the slope, out of sight of the men in the valley. And now the twang of an unseen bow broke the painful stillness. With a strangled gasp the Roman flung his hands high, and as the steed reared, he pitched headlong, transfixed by a long black arrow that had flashed from the heather. A stocky dwarf sprang out of nowhere, seemingly, and seized the bridle, quieting the snorting horse, and leading it down the slope. At the fall of the Roman, short crooked men rose like a sudden flight of birds from the grass and Cormac saw the flash of a knife. Then with unreal suddenness all had subsided. Slayers and slain were unseen and only the still-waving heather marked the grim deed.

The Gael looked back into the valley. The three who had ridden over the eastern ridge had not come back and Cormac knew they never would. Evidently the other scouts had borne word that only a small band of warriors was ready to dispute the passage of the legionaries. Now the head of the column was almost below him and he thrilled at the sight of these men who were doomed, swinging along with their superb arrogance. And the sight of their splendid armor, their hawk-like faces and perfect discipline awed him as much as it is possible for a Gael to be awed.

Twelve hundred men in heavy armor who marched as one so that the ground shook to their tread! Most of them were of middle height, with powerful chests and shoulders and bronzed faces – hard-bitten veterans of a hundred campaigns. Cormac noted their javelins, short keen swords and heavy shields; their gleaming armor and crested helmets, the eagles on the standards. These were the men beneath whose tread the world had shaken and empires crumbled! Not all were Latins; there were Romanized Britons among them and one century or hundred was composed of huge yellow-haired men – Gauls and Germans, who fought for Rome as fiercely as did the native-born, and hated their wilder kinsmen more savagely.

On each side was a swarm of cavalry, outriders, and the column was flanked by archers and slingers. A number of lumbering wagons carried the supplies of the army. Cormac saw the commander riding in his place – a tall man with a lean, imperious face, evident even at that distance. Marcus Sulius – the Gael knew him by repute.

A deep-throated roar rose from the legionaries as they approached their foes. Evidently they intended to slice their way through and continue without a pause, for the column moved implacably on. Whom the gods destroy they first make mad – Cormac had never heard the phrase but it came to him that the great Sulius was a fool. Roman arrogance! Marcus was used to lashing the cringing peoples of a decadent East; little he guessed of the iron in these western races.

A group of cavalry detached itself and raced into the mouth of the gorge, but it was only a gesture. With loud jeering shouts they wheeled three spears length away and cast their javelins, which rattled harmlessly on the overlapping shields of the silent Northmen. But their leader dared too much; swinging in, he leaned from his saddle and thrust at Kull's face. The great shield turned the lance and Kull struck back as a snake strikes; the ponderous mace crushed helmet and head like an eggshell, and the very steed went to its knees from the shock of that terrible blow. From the Northmen went up a short fierce roar, and the Picts beside them howled exultantly and loosed their arrows among the retreating horsemen. First blood for the people of the heather! The oncoming Romans shouted vengefully and quickened their pace as the frightened horse raced by, a ghastly travesty of a man, foot caught in the stirrup, trailing beneath the pounding hoofs.

Now the first line of the legionaries, compressed because of the narrowness of the gorge, crashed against the solid wall of shields – crashed and recoiled upon itself. The shield-wall had not shaken an inch. This was the first time the Roman legions had met with that unbreakable formation – that oldest of all Aryan battle-lines – the ancestor of the Spartan regiment – the Theban phalanx – the Macedonian formation – the English square.

Shield crashed on shield and the short Roman sword sought for an opening in that iron wall. Viking spears bristling in solid ranks above, thrust and reddened; heavy axes chopped down, shearing through iron, flesh and bone.

Cormac saw Kull, looming above the stocky Romans in the forefront of the fray, dealing blows like thunderbolts. A burly centurion rushed in, shield held high, stabbing upward. The iron mace crashed terribly, shivering the sword, rending the shield apart, shattering the helmet, crushing the skull down between the shoulders – in a single blow.

The front line of the Romans bent like a steel bar about the wedge, as the legionaries sought to struggle through the gorge on each side and surround their opposers. But the pass was too narrow; crouching close against the steep walls the Picts drove their black arrows in a hail of death. At this range the heavy shafts tore through shield and corselet, transfixing the armored men. The front line of battle rolled back, red and broken, and the Northmen trod their few dead underfoot to close the gaps their fall had made. Stretched the full width of their front lay a thin line of shattered forms – the red spray of the tide which had broken upon them in vain.

Cormac had leaped to his feet, waving his arms. Domnail and his men broke cover at the signal and came galloping up the slope, lining the ridge. Cormac mounted the horse brought him and glanced impatiently across the narrow vale. No sign of life appeared on the eastern ridge. Where was Bran – and the Britons?

Down in the valley, the legions, angered at the unexpected opposition of the paltry force in front of them, but not suspicious, were forming in more compact body. The wagons which had halted were lumbering on again and the whole column was once more in motion as if it intended to crash through by sheer weight. With the Gaulish century in the forefront, the legionaries were advancing again in the attack. This time, with the full force of twelve hundred men behind, the charge would batter down the resistance of Kull's warriors like a heavy ram; would stamp them down, sweep over their red ruins. Cormac's men trembled in impatience. Suddenly Marcus Sulius turned and gazed westward, where the line of horsemen was etched against the sky. Even at that distance Cormac saw his face pale. The Roman at last realized the metal of the men he faced, and that he had walked into a trap. Surely in that moment there flashed a chaotic picture through his brain – defeat – disgrace – red ruin!

It was too late to retreat – too late to form into a defensive square with the wagons for barricade. There was but one possible way out, and Marcus, crafty general in spite of his recent blunder, took it. Cormac heard his voice cut like a clarion through the din, and though he did not understand the words, he knew that the Roman was shouting for his men to smite that knot of Northmen like a blast – to hack their way through and out of the trap before it could close!

Now the legionaries, aware of their desperate plight, flung themselves headlong and terribly on their foes. The shield-wall rocked, but it gave not an inch. The wild faces of the Gauls and the hard brown Italian faces glared over locked shields into the blazing eyes of the North. Shields touching, they smote and slew and died in a red storm of slaughter, where crimsoned axes rose and fell and dripping spears broke on notched swords.

Where in God's name was Bran with his chariots? A few minutes more would spell the doom of every man who held that pass. Already they were falling fast, though they locked their ranks closer and held like iron. Those wild men of the North were dying in their tracks; and looming among their golden heads the black lion-mane of Kull shone like a symbol of slaughter, and his reddened mace showered a ghastly rain as it splashed brains and blood like water.

Something snapped in Cormac's brain.

"These men will die while we wait for Bran's signal!" he shouted. "On! Follow me into Hell, sons of Gael!"

A wild roar answered him, and loosing rein he shot down the slope with five hundred yelling riders plunging headlong after him. And even at that moment a storm of arrows swept the valley from either side like a dark cloud and the terrible clamor of the Picts split the skies. And over the eastern ridge, like a sudden burst of rolling thunder on Judgment Day, rushed the war-chariots. Headlong down the slope they roared, foam flying from the horses' distended nostrils, frantic feet scarcely seeming to touch the ground, making naught of the tall heather. In the foremost chariot, with his dark eyes blazing, crouched Bran Mak Morn, and in all of them the naked Britons were screaming and lashing as if possessed by demons. Behind the flying chariots came the Picts, howling like wolves and loosing their arrows as they ran. The heather belched them forth from all sides in a dark wave.

So much Cormac saw in chaotic glimpses during that wild ride down the slopes. A wave of cavalry swept between him and the main line of the column. Three long leaps ahead of his men, the Gaelic prince met the spears of the Roman riders. The first lance turned on his buckler, and rising in his stirrups he smote downward, cleaving his man from shoulder to breastbone. The next Roman flung a javelin that killed Domnail, but at that instant Cormac's steed crashed into his, breast to breast, and the lighter horse rolled headlong under the shock, flinging his rider beneath the pounding hoofs.

Then the whole blast of the Gaelic charge smote the Roman cavalry, shattering it, crashing and rolling it down and under. Over its red ruins Cormac's yelling demons struck the heavy Roman infantry, and the whole line reeled at the shock. Swords and axes flashed up and down and the force of their rush carried them deep into the massed ranks. Here, checked, they swayed and strove. Javelins thrust, swords flashed upward, bringing down horse and rider, and greatly outnumbered, leaguered on every side, the Gaels had perished among their foes, but at that instant, from the other side the crashing chariots smote the Roman ranks. In one long line they struck almost simultaneously, and at the moment of impact the charioteers wheeled their horses side-long and raced parallel down the ranks, shearing men down like the mowing of wheat. Hundreds died on those curving blades in that moment, and leaping from the chariots, screaming like blood-mad wildcats, the British swordsmen flung themselves upon the spears of the legionaries, hacking madly with their two-handed swords. Crouching, the Picts drove their arrows point-blank and then sprang in to slash and thrust. Maddened with the sight of victory, these wild peoples were like wounded tigers, feeling no wounds, and dying on their feet with their last gasp a snarl of fury.

But the battle was not over yet. Dazed, shattered, their formation broken and nearly half their number down already, the Romans fought back with desperate fury. Hemmed in on all sides they slashed and smote singly, or in small clumps, fought back to back, archers, slingers, horsemen and heavy legionaries mingled into a chaotic mass. The confusion was complete, but not the victory. Those bottled in the gorge still hurled themselves upon the red axes that barred their way, while the massed and serried battle thundered behind them. From one side Cormac's Gaels raged and slashed; from the other chariots swept back and forth, retiring and returning like iron whirlwinds. There was no retreat, for the Picts had flung a cordon across the way they had come, and having cut the throats of the camp followers and possessed themselves of the wagons, they sent their shafts in a storm of death into the rear of the shattered column. Those long black arrows pierced armor and bone, nailing men together. Yet the slaughter was not all on one side. Picts died beneath the lightning thrust of javelin and shortsword, Gaels pinned beneath their falling horses were hewed to pieces, and chariots, cut loose from their horses, were deluged with the blood of the charioteers.

And at the narrow head of the valley still the battle surged and eddied. Great gods – thought Cormac, glancing between lightning-like blows – do these men still hold the gorge? Aye! They held it! A tenth of their original number, dying on their feet, they still held back the frantic charges of the dwindling legionaries.

Over all the field went up the roar and the clash of arms, and birds of prey, swift-flying out of the sunset, circled above. Cormac, striving to reach Marcus Sulius through the press, saw the Roman's horse sink under him, and the rider rise alone in a waste of foes. He saw the Roman sword flash thrice, dealing a death at each blow; then from the thickest of the fray bounded a terrible figure. It was Bran Mak Morn, stained from head to foot. He cast away his broken sword as he ran, drawing a dirk. The Roman struck, but the Pictish king was under the thrust, and gripping the sword-wrist, he drove the dirk again and again through the gleaming armor.

A mighty roar went up as Marcus died, and Cormac, with a shout, rallied the remnants of his force about him and, striking in the spurs, burst through the shattered lines and rode full speed for the other end of the valley.

But as he approached he saw that he was too late. As they had lived, so had they died, those fierce sea-wolves, with their faces to the foe and their broken weapons red in their hands. In a grim and silent band they lay, even in death preserving some of the shield-wall formation. Among them, in front of them and all about them lay high-heaped the bodies of those who had sought to break them, in vain. *They had not given back a foot!* To the last man, they had died in their tracks. Nor were there any left to stride over their torn shapes; those Romans who had escaped the Viking axes had been struck down by the shafts of the Picts and swords of the Gaels from behind.

Yet this part of the battle was not over. High up on the steep western slope Cormac saw the ending of that drama. A group of Gauls in the armor of Rome pressed upon a single man – a black-haired giant on whose head gleamed a golden crown. There was iron in these men, as well as in the man who had held them to their fate. They were doomed – their comrades were being slaughtered behind them – but before their turn came they would at least have the life of the black-haired chief who had led the golden-haired men of the North.

Pressing upon him from three sides they had forced him slowly back up the steep gorge wall, and the crumpled bodies that stretched along his retreat showed how fiercely every foot of the way had been contested. Here on this steep it was task enough to keep one's footing alone; yet these men at once climbed and fought. Kull's shield and the huge mace were gone, and the great sword in his right hand was dyed crimson. His mail, wrought with a forgotten art, now hung in shreds, and blood streamed from a hundred wounds on limbs, head and body. But his eyes still blazed with the battle-joy and his wearied arm still drove the mighty blade in strokes of death.

But Cormac saw that the end would come before they could reach him. Now at the very crest of the steep, a hedge of points menaced the strange king's life, and even his iron strength was ebbing. Now he split the skull of a huge warrior and the backstroke shore through the neck-cords of another; reeling under a very rain of swords he struck again and his victim dropped at his feet, cleft to the breastbone. Then, even as a dozen swords rose above the staggering Atlantean for the death stroke, a strange thing happened. The sun was sinking into the western sea; all the heather swam red like an ocean of blood. Etched in the dying sun, as he had first appeared, Kull stood, and then, like a mist lifting, a mighty vista opened behind the reeling king. Cormac's astounded eyes caught a fleeting gigantic glimpse of other climes and spheres – as if mirrored in summer clouds he saw, instead of the heather hills stretching away to the sea, a dim and mighty land of blue mountains and gleaming quiet lakes – the golden, purple and sapphirean spires and towering walls of a mighty city such as the earth has not known for many a drifting age.

Then like the fading of a mirage it was gone, but the Gauls on the high slope had dropped their weapons and stared like men dazed – *For the man called Kull had vanished and there was no trace of his going!*

As in a daze Cormac turned his steed and rode back across the trampled field. His horse's hoofs splashed in lakes of blood and clanged against the helmets of dead men. Across the valley the shout of victory was thundering. Yet all seemed shadowy and strange. A shape was striding across the torn corpses and Cormac was dully aware that it was Bran. The Gael swung from his horse and fronted the king. Bran was weaponless and gory; blood trickled from gashes on brow, breast and limb; what armor he had worn was clean hacked away and a cut had shorn halfway through his iron crown. But the red jewel still gleamed unblemished like a star of slaughter.

"It is in my mind to slay you," said the Gael heavily and like a man speaking in a daze, "for the blood of brave men is on your head. Had you given the signal to charge sooner, some would have lived."

Bran folded his arms; his eyes were haunted. "Strike if you will; I am sick of slaughter. It is a cold mead, this kinging it. A king must gamble with men's lives and naked swords. The lives of all my people were at stake; I sacrificed the Northmen – yes; and my heart is sore within me, for they were men! But had I given the order when you would have desired, all might have gone awry. The Romans were not yet massed in the narrow mouth of the gorge, and might have had time and space to form their ranks again and beat us off. I waited until the last moment – and the rovers died. A king belongs to his people, and can not let either his own feelings or the lives of men influence him. Now my people are saved; but my heart is cold in my breast."

Cormac wearily dropped his sword-point to the ground.

"You are a born king of men, Bran," said the Gaelic prince.

Bran's eyes roved the field. A mist of blood hovered over all, where the victorious barbarians were looting the dead, while those Romans who had escaped slaughter by throwing down their swords and now stood under guard, looked on with hot smoldering eyes.

"My kingdom – my people – are saved," said Bran wearily. "They will come from the heather by the thousands and when Rome moves against us again, she will meet a solid nation. But I am weary. What of Kull?"

"My eyes and brain were mazed with battle," answered Cormac. "I thought to see him vanish like a ghost into the sunset. I will seek his body."

"Seek not for him," said Bran. "Out of the sunrise he came – into the sunset he has gone. Out of the mists of the ages he came to us, and back into the mists of the eons has he returned – to his own kingdom."

Cormac turned away; night was gathering. Gonar stood like a white specter before him.

"To his own kingdom," echoed the wizard. "Time and Space are naught. Kull has returned to his own kingdom – his own crown – his own age."

"Then he was a ghost?"

"Did you not feel the grip of his solid hand? Did you not hear his voice – see him eat and drink, laugh and slay and bleed?"

Still Cormac stood like one in a trance.

"Then if it be possible for a man to pass from one age into one yet unborn, or come forth from a century dead and forgotten, whichever you will, with his flesh-and-*blood body and his arms – then he is as mortal as he was in his own day. Is Kull dead,* then?"

"He died a hundred thousand years ago, as men reckon time," answered the wizard, "but in his own age. He died not from the swords of the Gauls of this age. Have we not heard in legends how the king of Valusia traveled into a strange, timeless land of the misty future ages, and there fought in a great battle? Why, so he did! A hundred thousand years ago, or today!

"And a hundred thousand years ago – or a moment agone! – Kull, king of Valusia, roused himself on the silken couch in his secret chamber and laughing, spoke to the first Gonar, saying: 'Ha, wizard, I have in truth dreamed strangely, for I went into a far clime and a far time in my visions, and fought for the king of a strange shadow-people!' And the great sorcerer smiled and pointed silently at the red, notched sword, and the torn mail and the many wounds that the king carried. And Kull, fully woken from his 'vision' and feeling the sting and the weakness of these yet bleeding wounds, fell silent and mazed, and all life and time and space seemed like a dream of ghosts to him, and he wondered thereat all the rest of his life. For the wisdom of the Eternities is denied even unto princes and Kull could no more understand what Gonar told him than you can understand my words."

"And then Kull lived despite his many wounds," said Cormac, "and has returned to the mists of silence and the centuries. Well – he thought us a dream; we thought him a ghost. And sure, life is but a web spun of ghosts and dreams and illusion, and it is in my mind that the kingdom which has this day been born of swords and slaughter in this howling valley is a thing no more solid than the foam of the bright sea."

Worms of the Earth

Chapter 1

"STRIKE in the nails, soldiers, and let our guest see the reality of our good Roman justice!"

The speaker wrapped his purple cloak closer about his powerful frame and settled back into his official chair, much as he might have settled back in his seat at the Circus Maximus to enjoy the clash of gladiatorial swords. Realization of power colored his every move. Whetted pride was necessary to Roman satisfaction, and Titus Sulla was justly proud; for he was military governor of Eboracum and answerable only to the emperor of Rome. He was a strongly built man of medium height, with the hawk-like features of the pure-bred Roman. Now a mocking smile curved his full lips, increasing the arrogance of his haughty aspect. Distinctly military in appearance, he wore the golden-scaled corselet and chased breastplate of his rank, with the short stabbing sword at his belt, and he held on his knee the silvered helmet with its plumed crest. Behind him stood a clump of impassive soldiers with shield and spear – blond titans from the Rhineland.

Before him was taking place the scene which apparently gave him so much real gratification – a scene common enough wherever stretched the far-flung boundaries of Rome. A rude cross lay flat upon the barren earth and on it was bound a man – half-naked, wild of aspect with his corded limbs, glaring eyes and shock of tangled hair. His executioners were Roman soldiers, and with heavy hammers they prepared to pin the victim's hands and feet to the wood with iron spikes.

Only a small group of men watched this ghastly scene, in the dread place of execution beyond the city walls: the governor and his watchful guards; a few young Roman officers; the man to whom Sulla had referred as "guest" and who stood like a bronze image, unspeaking. Beside the gleaming splendor of the Roman, the quiet garb of this man seemed drab, almost somber.

He was dark, but he did not resemble the Latins around him. There was about him none of the warm, almost Oriental sensuality of the Mediterranean which colored their features. The blond barbarians behind Sulla's chair were less unlike the man in facial outline than were the Romans. Not his were the full curving red lips, nor the rich waving locks suggestive of the Greek. Nor was his dark complexion the rich olive of the south; rather it was the bleak darkness of the north. The whole aspect of the man vaguely suggested the shadowed mists, the gloom, the cold and the icy winds of the naked northern lands. Even his black eyes were savagely cold, like black fires burning through fathoms of ice.

His height was only medium but there was something about him which transcended mere physical bulk – a certain fierce innate vitality, comparable only to that of a wolf or a panther. In every line of his supple, compact body, as well as in his coarse straight hair and thin lips, this was evident – in the hawk-like set of the head on the corded neck, in the broad square shoulders, in the deep chest, the lean loins, the narrow feet. Built with the savage economy of a panther, he was an image of dynamic potentialities, pent in with iron self-control.

At his feet crouched one like him in complexion – but there the resemblance ended. This other was a stunted giant, with gnarly limbs, thick body, a low sloping brow and an expression of dull ferocity, now clearly mixed with fear. If the man on the cross resembled, in a tribal way, the man Titus Sulla called guest, he far more resembled the stunted crouching giant.

"Well, Partha Mac Othna," said the governor with studied effrontery, "when you return to your tribe, you will have a tale to tell of the justice of Rome, who rules the south."

"I will have a tale," answered the other in a voice which betrayed no emotion, just as his dark face, schooled to immobility, showed no evidence of the maelstrom in his soul.

"Justice to all under the rule of Rome," said Sulla. "Pax Romana! Reward for virtue, punishment for wrong!" He laughed inwardly at his own black hypocrisy, then continued: "You see, emissary of Pictland, how swiftly Rome punishes the transgressor."

"I see," answered the Pict in a voice which strongly-curbed anger made deep with menace, "that the subject of a foreign king is dealt with as though he were a Roman slave."

"He has been tried and condemned in an unbiased court," retorted Sulla.

"Aye! And the accuser was a Roman, the witnesses Roman, the judge Roman! He committed murder? In a moment of fury he struck down a Roman merchant who cheated, tricked and robbed him, and to injury added insult – aye, and a blow! Is his king but a dog, that Rome crucifies his subjects at will, condemned by Roman courts? Is his king too weak or foolish to do justice, were he informed and formal charges brought against the offender?"

"Well," said Sulla cynically, "you may inform Bran Mak Morn yourself. Rome, my friend, makes no account of her actions to barbarian kings. When savages come among us, let them act with discretion or suffer the consequences."

The Pict shut his iron jaws with a snap that told Sulla further badgering would elicit no reply. The Roman made a gesture to the executioners. One of them seized a spike and placing it against the thick wrist of the victim, smote heavily. The iron point sank deep through the flesh, crunching against the bones. The lips of the man on the cross writhed, though no moan escaped him. As a trapped wolf fights against his cage, the bound victim instinctively wrenched and struggled. The veins swelled in his temples, sweat beaded his low forehead, the muscles in arms and legs writhed and knotted. The hammers fell in inexorable strokes, driving the cruel points deeper and deeper, through wrists and ankles; blood flowed in a black river over the hands that held the spikes, staining the wood of the cross, and the splintering of bones was distinctly heard. Yet the sufferer made no outcry, though his blackened lips writhed back until the gums were visible, and his shaggy head jerked involuntarily from side to side.

The man called Partha Mac Othna stood like an iron image, eyes burning from an inscrutable face, his whole body hard as iron from the tension of his control. At his feet crouched his misshapen servant, hiding his face from the grim sight, his arms locked about his master's knees. Those arms gripped like steel and under his breath the fellow mumbled ceaselessly as if in invocation.

The last stroke fell; the cords were cut from arm and leg, so that the man would hang supported by the nails alone. He had ceased his struggling that only twisted the spikes in his agonizing wounds. His bright black eyes, unglazed, had not left the face of the man called Partha Mac Othna; in them lingered a desperate shadow of hope. Now the soldiers lifted the cross and set the end of it in the hole prepared, stamped the dirt about it to hold it erect. The Pict hung in midair, suspended by the nails in his flesh, but still no sound escaped his lips. His eyes still hung on the somber face of the emissary, but the shadow of hope was fading.

"He'll live for days!" said Sulla cheerfully. "These Picts are harder than cats to kill! I'll keep a guard of ten soldiers watching night and day to see that no one takes him down before he dies. Ho, there, Valerius, in honor of our esteemed neighbor, King Bran Mak Morn, give him a cup of wine!"

With a laugh the young officer came forward, holding a brimming wine cup, and rising on his toes, lifted it to the parched lips of the sufferer. In the black eyes flared a red wave of unquenchable hatred; writhing his head aside to avoid even touching the cup, he spat full into the young Roman's eyes. With a curse Valerius dashed the cup to the ground, and before any could halt him, wrenched out his sword and sheathed it in the man's body.

Sulla rose with an imperious exclamation of anger; the man called Partha Mac Othna had started violently, but he bit his lip and said nothing. Valerius seemed somewhat surprized at him as he sullenly cleansed his sword. The act had been instinctive, following the insult to Roman pride, the one thing unbearable.

"Give up your sword, young sir!" exclaimed Sulla. "Centurion Publius, place him under arrest. A few days in a cell with stale bread and water will teach you to curb your patrician pride in matters dealing with the will of the empire. What, you young fool, do you not realize that you could not have made the dog a more kindly gift? Who would not rather desire a quick death on the sword than the slow agony on the cross? Take him away. And you, centurion, see that guards remain at the cross so that the body is not cut down until the ravens pick bare the bones. Partha Mac Othna, I go to a banquet at the house of Demetrius – will you not accompany me?"

The emissary shook his head, his eyes fixed on the limp form which sagged on the black-stained cross. He made no reply. Sulla smiled sardonically, then rose and strode away, followed by his secretary who bore the gilded chair ceremoniously, and by the stolid soldiers, with whom walked Valerius, head sunken.

The man called Partha Mac Othna flung a wide fold of his cloak about his shoulder, halted a moment to gaze at the grim cross with its burden, darkly etched against the crimson sky, where the clouds of night were gathering. Then he stalked away, followed by his silent servant.

Chapter 2

In an inner chamber of Eboracum, the man called Partha Mac Othna paced tigerishly to and fro. His sandaled feet made no sound on the marble tiles.

"Grom!" he turned to the gnarled servant. "Well I know why you held my knees so tightly – why you muttered aid of the Moon-Woman – you feared I would lose my self-control and make a mad attempt to succor that poor wretch. By the gods, I believe that was what the dog Roman wished – his iron-cased watchdogs watched me narrowly, I know, and his baiting was harder to bear than ordinarily.

"Gods black and white, dark and light!" He shook his clenched fists above his head in the black gust of his passion. "That I should stand by and see a man of mine butchered on a Roman cross – without justice and with no more trial than that farce! Black gods of R'lyeh, even you would I invoke to the ruin and destruction of those butchers! I swear by the Nameless Ones, men shall die howling for that deed, and Rome shall cry out as a woman in the dark who treads upon an adder!"

"He knew you, master," said Grom.

The other dropped his head and covered his eyes with a gesture of savage pain.

"His eyes will haunt me when I lie dying. Aye, he knew me, and almost until the last, I read in his eyes the hope that I might aid him. Gods and devils, is Rome to butcher my people beneath my very eyes? Then I am not king but dog!"

"Not so loud, in the name of all the gods!" exclaimed Grom in affright. "Did these Romans suspect you were Bran Mak Morn, they would nail you on a cross beside that other."

"They will know it ere long," grimly answered the king. "Too long I have lingered here in the guise of an emissary, spying upon mine enemies. They have thought to play with me, these Romans, masking their contempt and scorn only under polished satire. Rome is courteous to barbarian ambassadors, they give us fine houses to live in, offer us slaves, pander to our lusts with women and gold and wine and games, but all the while they laugh at us; their very courtesy is an insult, and sometimes – as today – their contempt discards all veneer. Bah! I've seen through their baitings – have remained imperturbably serene and swallowed their studied insults. But this – by the fiends of Hell, this is beyond human endurance! My people look to me; if I fail them – if I fail even one – even the lowest of my people, who will aid them? To whom shall they turn? By the gods, I'll answer the gibes of these Roman dogs with black shaft and trenchant steel!"

"And the chief with the plumes?" Grom meant the governor and his gutturals thrummed with the blood-lust. "He dies?" He flicked out a length of steel.

Bran scowled. "Easier said than done. He dies – but how may I reach him? By day his German guards keep at his back; by night they stand at door and window. He has many enemies, Romans as well as barbarians. Many a Briton would gladly slit his throat."

Grom seized Bran's garment, stammering as fierce eagerness broke the bonds of his inarticulate nature.

"Let me go, master! My life is worth nothing. I will cut him down in the midst of his warriors!"

Bran smiled fiercely and clapped his hand on the stunted giant's shoulder with a force that would have felled a lesser man.

"Nay, old war-dog, I have too much need of thee! You shall not throw your life away uselessly. Sulla would read the intent in your eyes, besides, and the javelins of his Teutons would be through you ere you could reach him. Not by the dagger in the dark will we strike this Roman, not by the venom in the cup nor the shaft from the ambush."

The king turned and paced the floor a moment, his head bent in thought. Slowly his eyes grew murky with a thought so fearful he did not speak it aloud to the waiting warrior.

"I have become somewhat familiar with the maze of Roman politics during my stay in this accursed waste of mud and marble," said he. "During a war on the Wall, Titus Sulla, as governor of this province, is supposed to hasten thither with his centuries. But this Sulla does not do; he is no coward, but the bravest avoid certain things – to each man, however bold, his own particular fear. So he sends in his place Caius Camillus, who in times of peace patrols the fens of the west, lest the Britons break over the border. And Sulla takes his place in the Tower of Trajan. Ha!"

He whirled and gripped Grom with steely fingers.

"Grom, take the red stallion and ride north! Let no grass grow under the stallion's hoofs! Ride to Cormac na

Connacht and tell him to sweep the frontier with sword and torch! Let his wild Gaels feast their fill of slaughter. After a time I will be with him. But for a time I have affairs in the west."

Grom's black eyes gleamed and he made a passionate gesture with his crooked hand – an instinctive move of savagery.

Bran drew a heavy bronze seal from beneath his tunic.

"This is my safe-conduct as an emissary to Roman courts," he said grimly. "It will open all gates between this house and Baal-dor. If any official questions you too closely – here!"

Lifting the lid of an iron-bound chest, Bran took out a small, heavy leather bag which he gave into the hands of the warrior.

"When all keys fail at a gate," said he, "try a golden key. Go now!"

There were no ceremonious farewells between the barbarian king and his barbarian vassal. Grom flung up his arm in a gesture of salute; then turning, he hurried out.

Bran stepped to a barred window and gazed out into the moonlit streets.

"Wait until the moon sets," he muttered grimly. "Then I'll take the road to – Hell! But before I go I have a debt to pay."

The stealthy clink of a hoof on the flags reached him.

"With the safe-conduct and gold, not even Rome can hold a Pictish reaver," muttered the king. "Now I'll sleep until the moon sets."

With a snarl at the marble frieze-work and fluted columns, as symbols of Rome, he flung himself down on a couch, from which he had long since impatiently torn the cushions and silk stuffs, as too soft for his hard body. Hate and the black passion of vengeance seethed in him, yet he went instantly to sleep. The first lesson he had learned in his bitter hard life was to snatch sleep any time he could, like a wolf that snatches sleep on the hunting trail. Generally his slumber was as light and dreamless as a panther's, but tonight it was otherwise.

He sank into fleecy gray fathoms of slumber and in a timeless, misty realm of shadows he met the tall, lean, white-bearded figure of old Gonar, the priest of the Moon, high counselor to the king. And Bran stood aghast, for Gonar's face was white as driven snow and he shook as with ague. Well might Bran stand appalled, for in all the years of his life he had never before seen Gonar the Wise show any sign of fear.

"What now, old one?" asked the king. "Goes all well in Baal-dor?"

"All is well in Baal-dor where my body lies sleeping," answered old Gonar. "Across the void I have come to battle with you for your soul. King, are you mad, this thought you have thought in your brain?"

"Gonar," answered Bran somberly, "this day I stood still and watched a man of mine die on the cross of Rome. What his name or his rank, I do not know. I do not care. He might have been a faithful unknown warrior of mine, he might have been an outlaw. I only know that he was mine; the first scents he knew were the scents of the heather; the first light he saw was the sunrise on the Pictish hills. He belonged to me, not to Rome. If punishment was just, then none but me should have dealt it. If he were to be tried, none but me should have been his judge. The same blood flowed in our veins; the same fire maddened our brains; in infancy we listened to the same old tales, and in youth we sang the same old songs. He was bound to my heartstrings, as every man and every woman and every child of Pictland is bound. It was mine to protect him; now it is mine to avenge him."

"But in the name of the gods, Bran," expostulated the wizard, "take your vengeance in another way! Return to the heather – mass your warriors – join with Cormac and his Gaels, and spread a sea of blood and flame the length of the great Wall!"

"All that I will do," grimly answered Bran. "But now – now – I will have a vengeance such as no Roman ever dreamed of! Ha, what do they know of the mysteries of this ancient isle, which sheltered strange life long before Rome rose from the marshes of the Tiber?"

"Bran, there are weapons too foul to use, even against Rome!"

Bran barked short and sharp as a jackal.

"Ha! There are no weapons I would not use against Rome! My back is at the wall. By the blood of the fiends, has Rome fought me fair? Bah! I am a barbarian king with a wolfskin mantle and an iron crown, fighting with my handful of bows and broken pikes against the queen of the world. What have I? The heather hills, the wattle huts, the spears of my shock-headed tribesmen! And I fight Rome – with her armored legions, her broad fertile plains and rich seas – her mountains and her rivers and her gleaming cities – her wealth, her steel, her gold, her mastery and her wrath. By steel and fire I will fight her – and by subtlety and treachery – by the thorn in the foot, the adder in the path, the venom in the cup, the dagger in the dark; aye," his voice sank somberly, "and by the worms of the earth!"

"But it is madness!" cried Gonar. "You will perish in the attempt you plan – you will go down to Hell and you will not return! What of your people then?"

"If I can not serve them I had better die," growled the king.

"But you can not even reach the beings you seek," cried Gonar. "For untold centuries they have dwelt apart. There is no door by which you can come to them. Long ago they severed the bonds that bound them to the world we know."

"Long ago," answered Bran somberly, "you told me that nothing in the universe was separated from the stream of Life – a saying the truth of which I have often seen evident. No race, no form of life but is close-knit somehow, by some manner, to the rest of Life and the world. Somewhere there is a thin link connecting those I seek to the world I know.

Somewhere there is a Door. And somewhere among the bleak fens of the west I will find it."

Stark horror flooded Gonar's eyes and he gave back crying, "Woe! Woe! Woe! to Pictdom! Woe to the unborn kingdom! Woe, black woe to the sons of men! Woe, woe, woe, woe!"

Bran awoke to a shadowed room and the starlight on the window-bars. The moon had sunk from sight though its glow was still faint above the house tops. Memory of his dream shook him and he swore beneath his breath.

Rising, he flung off cloak and mantle, donning a light shirt of black mesh-mail, and girding on sword and dirk. Going again to the iron-bound chest he lifted several compact bags and emptied the clinking contents into the leathern pouch at his girdle. Then wrapping his wide cloak about him, he silently left the house. No servants there were to spy on him – he had impatiently refused the offer of slaves which it was Rome's policy to furnish her barbarian emissaries. Gnarled Grom had attended to all Bran's simple needs.

The stables fronted on the courtyard. A moment's groping in the dark and he placed his hand over a great stallion's nose, checking the nicker of recognition. Working without a light he swiftly bridled and saddled the great brute, and went through the courtyard into a shadowy side street, leading him. The moon was setting, the border of floating shadows widening along the western wall. Silence lay on the marble palaces and mud hovels of Eboracum under the cold stars.

Bran touched the pouch at his girdle, which was heavy with minted gold that bore the stamp of Rome. He had come to Eboracum posing as an emissary of Pictdom, to act the spy. But being a barbarian, he had not been able to play his part in aloof formality and sedate dignity. He retained a crowded memory of wild feasts where wine flowed in fountains; of white-bosomed Roman women, who, sated with civilized lovers, looked with something more than favor on a virile barbarian; of gladiatorial games; and of other games where dice clicked and spun and tall stacks of gold changed hands. He had drunk deeply and gambled recklessly, after the manner of barbarians, and he had had a remarkable run of luck, due possibly to the indifference with which he won or lost. Gold to the Pict was so much dust, flowing through his fingers. In his land there was no need of it. But he had learned its power in the boundaries of civilization.

Almost under the shadow of the northwestern wall he saw ahead of him loom the great watchtower which was connected with and reared above the outer wall. One corner of the castle-like fortress, farthest from the wall, served as a dungeon. Bran left his horse standing in a dark alley, with the reins hanging on the ground, and stole like a prowling wolf into the shadows of the fortress.

The young officer Valerius was awakened from a light, unquiet sleep by a stealthy sound at the barred window. He sat up, cursing softly under his breath as the faint starlight which etched the window-bars fell across the bare stone floor and reminded him of his disgrace. Well, in a few days, he ruminated, he'd be well out of it; Sulla would not be too harsh on a man with such high connections; then let any man or woman gibe at him! Damn that insolent Pict! But wait, he thought suddenly, remembering: what of the sound which had roused him?

"Hsssst!" it was a voice from the window.

Why so much secrecy? It could hardly be a foe – yet, why should it be a friend? Valerius rose and crossed his cell, coming close to the window. Outside all was dim in the starlight and he made out but a shadowy form close to the window.

"Who are you?" he leaned close against the bars, straining his eyes into the gloom.

His answer was a snarl of wolfish laughter, a long flicker of steel in the starlight. Valerius reeled away from the window and crashed to the floor, clutching his throat, gurgling horribly as he tried to scream. Blood gushed through his fingers, forming about his twitching body a pool that reflected the dim starlight dully and redly.

Outside Bran glided away like a shadow, without pausing to peer into the cell. In another minute the guards would round the corner on their regular routine. Even now he heard the measured tramp of their iron-clad feet. Before they came in sight he had vanished and they clumped stolidly by the cell-window with no intimation of the corpse that lay on the floor within.

Bran rode to the small gate in the western wall, unchallenged by the sleepy watch. What fear of foreign invasion in Eboracum? – and certain well organized thieves and women-stealers made it profitable for the watchmen not to be too vigilant. But the single guardsman at the western gate – his fellows lay drunk in a nearby brothel – lifted his spear and bawled for Bran to halt and give an account of himself. Silently the Pict reined closer. Masked in the dark cloak, he seemed dim and indistinct to the Roman, who was only aware of the glitter of his cold eyes in the gloom. But Bran held up his hand against the starlight and the soldier caught the gleam of gold; in the other hand he saw a long sheen of steel. The soldier understood, and he did not hesitate between the choice of a golden bribe or a battle to the death with this unknown rider who was apparently a barbarian of some sort. With a grunt he lowered his spear and swung the gate open. Bran rode through, casting a handful of coins to the Roman. They fell about his feet in a golden shower, clinking against the flags. He bent in greedy haste to retrieve them and Bran Mak Morn rode westward like a flying ghost in the night.

Chapter 3

Into the dim fens of the west came Bran Mak Morn. A cold wind breathed across the gloomy waste and against the gray sky a few herons flapped heavily. The long reeds and marsh-grass waved in broken undulations and out across the desolation of the wastes a few still meres reflected the dull light. Here and there rose curiously regular hillocks above the general levels, and gaunt against the somber sky Bran saw a marching line of upright monoliths – menhirs, reared by what nameless hands?

As a faint blue line to the west lay the foothills that beyond the horizon grew to the wild mountains of Wales where dwelt still wild Celtic tribes – fierce blue-eyed men that knew not the yoke of Rome. A row of well-garrisoned watchtowers held them in check. Even now, far away across the moors, Bran glimpsed the unassailable keep men called the Tower of Trajan.

These barren wastes seemed the dreary accomplishment of desolation, yet human life was not utterly lacking. Bran met the silent men of the fen, reticent, dark of eye and hair, speaking a strange mixed tongue whose long-blended elements had forgotten their pristine separate sources. Bran recognized a certain kinship in these people to himself, but he looked on them with the scorn of a pure-blooded patrician for men of mixed strains.

Not that the common people of Caledonia were altogether pure-blooded; they got their stocky bodies and massive limbs from a primitive Teutonic race which had found its way into the northern tip of the isle even before the Celtic conquest of Britain was completed, and had been absorbed by the Picts. But the chiefs of Bran's folk had kept their blood from foreign taint since the beginnings of time, and he himself was a pure-bred Pict of the Old Race. But these fenmen, overrun repeatedly by British, Gaelic and Roman conquerors, had assimilated blood of each, and in the process almost forgotten their original language and lineage.

For Bran came of a race that was very old, which had spread over western Europe in one vast Dark Empire, before the coming of the Aryans, when the ancestors of the Celts, the Hellenes and the Germans were one primal people, before the days of tribal splitting-off and westward drift.

Only in Caledonia, Bran brooded, had his people resisted the flood of Aryan conquest. He had heard of a Pictish people called Basques, who in the crags of the Pyrenees called themselves an unconquered race; but he knew that they had paid tribute for centuries to the ancestors of the Gaels, before these Celtic conquerors abandoned their mountain-realm and set sail for Ireland. Only the Picts of Caledonia had remained free, and they had been scattered into small feuding tribes – he was the first acknowledged king in five hundred years – the beginning of a new dynasty – no, a revival of an ancient dynasty under a new name. In the very teeth of Rome he dreamed his dreams of empire.

He wandered through the fens, seeking a Door. Of his quest he said nothing to the dark-eyed fenmen. They told him news that drifted from mouth to mouth – a tale of war in the north, the skirl of war-pipes along the winding Wall, of gathering-fires in the heather, of flame and smoke and rapine and the glutting of Gaelic swords in the crimson sea of slaughter. The eagles of the legions were moving northward and the ancient road resounded to the measured tramp of the iron-clad feet. And Bran, in the fens of the west, laughed, well pleased.

In Eboracum, Titus Sulla gave secret word to seek out the Pictish emissary with the Gaelic name who had been under suspicion, and who had vanished the night young Valerius was found dead in his cell with his throat ripped out. Sulla felt that this sudden bursting flame of war on the Wall was connected closely with his execution of a condemned Pictish criminal, and he set his spy system to work, though he felt sure that Partha Mac Othna was by this time far beyond his reach. He prepared to march from Eboracum, but he did not accompany the considerable force of legionaries which he sent north. Sulla was a brave man, but each man has his own dread, and Sulla's was Cormac na Connacht, the black-haired prince of the Gaels, who had sworn to cut out the governor's heart and eat it raw. So Sulla rode with his ever-present bodyguard, westward, where lay the Tower of Trajan with its warlike commander, Caius Camillus, who enjoyed nothing more than taking his superior's place when the red waves of war washed at the foot of the Wall. Devious politics, but the legate of Rome seldom visited this far isle, and what of his wealth and intrigues, Titus Sulla was the highest power in Britain.

And Bran, knowing all this, patiently waited his coming, in the deserted hut in which he had taken up his abode.

One gray evening he strode on foot across the moors, a stark figure, blackly etched against the dim crimson fire of the sunset. He felt the incredible antiquity of the slumbering land, as he walked like the last man on the day after the end of the world. Yet at last he saw a token of human life – a drab hut of wattle and mud, set in the reedy breast of the fen.

A woman greeted him from the open door and Bran's somber eyes narrowed with a dark suspicion. The woman was not old, yet the evil wisdom of ages was in her eyes; her garments were ragged and scanty, her black locks tangled and unkempt, lending her an aspect of wildness well in keeping with her grim surroundings. Her red lips laughed but there was no mirth in her laughter, only a hint of mockery, and under the lips her teeth showed sharp and pointed like fangs.

"Enter, master," said she, "if you do not fear to share the roof of the witch-woman of Dagon-moor!"

Bran entered silently and sat him down on a broken bench while the woman busied herself with the scanty meal cooking over an open fire on the squalid hearth. He studied her lithe, almost serpentine motions, the ears which were almost pointed, the yellow eyes which slanted curiously.

"What do you seek in the fens, my lord?" she asked, turning toward him with a supple twist of her whole body.

"I seek a Door," he answered, chin resting on his fist. "I have a song to sing to the worms of the earth!"

She started upright, a jar falling from her hands to shatter on the hearth.

"This is an ill saying, even spoken in chance," she stammered.

"I speak not by chance but by intent," he answered.

She shook her head. "I know not what you mean."

"Well you know," he returned. "Aye, you know well! My race is very old – they reigned in Britain before the nations of the Celts and the Hellenes were born out of the womb of peoples. But my people were not first in Britain. By the mottles on your skin, by the slanting of your eyes, by the taint in your veins, I speak with full knowledge and meaning."

Awhile she stood silent, her lips smiling but her face inscrutable.

"Man, are you mad," she asked, "that in your madness you come seeking that from which strong men fled screaming in old times?"

"I seek a vengeance," he answered, "that can be accomplished only by Them I seek."

She shook her head.

"You have listened to a bird singing; you have dreamed empty dreams."

"I have heard a viper hiss," he growled, "and I do not dream. Enough of this weaving of words. I came seeking a link between two worlds; I have found it."

"I need lie to you no more, man of the North," answered the woman. "They you seek still dwell beneath the sleeping hills. They have drawn apart, farther and farther from the world you know."

"But they still steal forth in the night to grip women straying on the moors," said he, his gaze on her slanted eyes. She laughed wickedly.

"What would you of me?"

"That you bring me to Them."

She flung back her head with a scornful laugh. His left hand locked like iron in the breast of her scanty garment and his right closed on his hilt. She laughed in his face.

"Strike and be damned, my northern wolf! Do you think that such life as mine is so sweet that I would cling to it as a babe to the breast?"

His hand fell away.

"You are right. Threats are foolish. I will buy your aid."

"How?" the laughing voice hummed with mockery.

Bran opened his pouch and poured into his cupped palm a stream of gold.

"More wealth than the men of the fen ever dreamed of."

Again she laughed. "What is this rusty metal to me? Save it for some white-breasted Roman woman who will play the traitor for you!"

"Name me a price!" he urged. "The head of an enemy–"

"By the blood in my veins, with its heritage of ancient hate, who is mine enemy but thee?" she laughed and springing, struck catlike. But her dagger splintered on the mail beneath his cloak and he flung her off with a loathsome flit of his wrist which tossed her sprawling across her grass-strewn bunk. Lying there she laughed up at him.

"I will name you a price, then, my wolf, and it may be in days to come you will curse the armor that broke Atla's dagger!" She rose and came close to him, her disquietingly long hands fastened fiercely into his cloak. "I will tell you, Black Bran, king of Caledon! Oh, I knew you when you came into my hut with your black hair and your cold eyes! I will lead you to the doors of Hell if you wish – and the price shall be the kisses of a king!

"What of my blasted and bitter life, I, whom mortal men loathe and fear? I have not known the love of men, the clasp of a strong arm, the sting of human kisses, I, Atla, the were-woman of the moors! What have I known but the lone winds of the fens, the dreary fire of cold sunsets, the whispering of the marsh grasses? – the faces that blink up at me in the waters of the meres, the foot-pad of night – things in the gloom, the glimmer of red eyes, the grisly murmur of nameless beings in the night!

"I am half-human, at least! Have I not known sorrow and yearning and crying wistfulness, and the drear ache of loneliness? Give to me, king – give me your fierce kisses and your hurtful barbarian's embrace. Then in the long drear years to come I shall not utterly eat out my heart in vain envy of the white-bosomed women of men; for I shall have a memory few of them can boast – the kisses of a king! One night of love, oh king, and I will guide you to the gates of Hell!"

Bran eyed her somberly; he reached forth and gripped her arm in his iron fingers. An involuntary shudder shook him at the feel of her sleek skin. He nodded slowly and drawing her close to him, forced his head down to meet her lifted lips.

Chapter 4

The cold gray mists of dawn wrapped King Bran like a clammy cloak. He turned to the woman whose slanted eyes gleamed in the gray gloom.

"Make good your part of the contract," he said roughly. "I sought a link between worlds, and in you I found it. I seek the one thing sacred to Them. It shall be the Key opening the Door that lies unseen between me and Them. Tell me how I can reach it."

"I will," the red lips smiled terribly. "Go to the mound men call Dagon's Barrow. Draw aside the stone that blocks the entrance and go under the dome of the mound. The floor of the chamber is made of seven great stones, six grouped about the seventh. Lift out the center stone – and you will see!"

"Will I find the Black Stone?" he asked.

"Dagon's Barrow is the Door to the Black Stone," she answered, "if you dare follow the Road."

"Will the symbol be well guarded?" He unconsciously loosened his blade in its sheath. The red lips curled mockingly.

"If you meet any on the Road you will die as no mortal man has died for long centuries. The Stone is not guarded, as men guard their treasures. Why should They guard what man has never sought? Perhaps They will be near, perhaps not. It is a chance you must take, if you wish the Stone. Beware, king of Pictdom! Remember it was your folk who, so long ago, cut the thread that bound Them to human life. They were almost human then – they overspread the land and knew the sunlight. Now they have drawn apart. They know not the sunlight and they shun the light of the moon. Even the starlight they hate. Far, far apart have they drawn, who might have been men in time, but for the spears of your ancestors."

The sky was overcast with misty gray, through which the sun shone coldly yellow when Bran came to Dagon's Barrow, a round hillock overgrown with rank grass of a curious fungoid appearance. On the eastern side of the mound showed the entrance of a crudely built stone tunnel which evidently penetrated the barrow. One great stone blocked the entrance to the tomb. Bran laid hold of the sharp edges and exerted all his strength. It held fast. He drew his sword and worked the blade between the blocking stone and the sill. Using the sword as a lever, he worked carefully, and managed to loosen the great stone and wrench it out. A foul charnel house scent flowed out of the aperture and the dim sunlight seemed less to illuminate the cavern-like opening than to be fouled by the rank darkness which clung there.

Sword in hand, ready for he knew not what, Bran groped his way into the tunnel, which was long and narrow, built up of heavy joined stones, and was too low for him to stand erect. Either his eyes became somewhat accustomed to the gloom, or the darkness was, after all, somewhat lightened by the sunlight filtering in through the entrance. At any rate he came into a round low chamber and was able to make out its general dome-like outline. Here, no doubt, in old times, had reposed the bones of him for whom the stones of the tomb had been joined and the earth heaped high above them; but now of those bones no vestige remained on the stone floor. And bending close and straining his eyes, Bran made out the strange, startlingly regular pattern of that floor: six well-cut slabs clustered about a seventh, six-sided stone.

He drove his sword-point into a crack and pried carefully. The edge of the central stone tilted slightly upward. A little work and he lifted it out and leaned it against the curving wall. Straining his eyes downward he saw only the gaping blackness of a dark well, with small, worn steps that led downward and out of sight. He did not hesitate. Though the skin between his shoulders crawled curiously, he swung himself into the abyss and felt the clinging blackness swallow him.

Groping downward, he felt his feet slip and stumble on steps too small for human feet. With one hand pressed hard against the side of the well he steadied himself, fearing a fall into unknown and unlighted depths. The steps were cut into solid rock, yet they were greatly worn away. The farther he progressed, the less like steps they became, mere bumps of worn stone. Then the direction of the shaft changed sharply. It still led down, but at a shallow slant down which he could walk, elbows braced against the hollowed sides, head bent low beneath the curved roof. The steps had ceased altogether and the stone felt slimy to the touch, like a serpent's lair. What beings, Bran wondered, had slithered up and down this slanting shaft, for how many centuries?

The tunnel narrowed until Bran found it rather difficult to shove through. He lay on his back and pushed himself along with his hands, feet first. Still he knew he was sinking deeper and deeper into the very guts of the earth; how far below the surface he was, he dared not contemplate. Then ahead a faint witch-fire gleam tinged the abysmal blackness. He grinned savagely and without mirth. If They he sought came suddenly upon him, how could he fight in that narrow shaft? But he had put the thought of personal fear behind him when he began this hellish quest. He crawled on, thoughtless of all else but his goal.

And he came at last into a vast space where he could stand upright. He could not see the roof of the place, but he got an impression of dizzying vastness. The blackness pressed in on all sides and behind him he could see the entrance to the shaft from which he had just emerged – a black well in the darkness. But in front of him a strange grisly radiance glowed about a grim altar built of human skulls. The source of that light he could not determine, but on the altar lay a sullen night-black object – the Black Stone!

Bran wasted no time in giving thanks that the guardians of the grim relic were nowhere near. He caught up the Stone, and gripping it under his left arm, crawled into the shaft. When a man turns his back on peril its clammy menace looms more grisly than when he advances upon it. So Bran, crawling back up the nighted shaft with his grisly prize, felt the darkness turn on him and slink behind him, grinning with dripping fangs. Clammy sweat beaded his flesh and he hastened to the best of his ability, ears strained for some stealthy sound to betray that fell shapes were at his heels. Strong shudders shook him, despite himself, and the short hair on his neck prickled as if a cold wind blew at his back.

When he reached the first of the tiny steps he felt as if he had attained to the outer boundaries of the mortal world. Up them he went, stumbling and slipping, and with a deep gasp of relief, came out into the tomb, whose spectral grayness seemed like the blaze of noon in comparison to the stygian depths he had just traversed. He replaced the central stone and strode into the light of the outer day, and never was the cold yellow light of the sun more grateful, as it dispelled the shadows of black-winged nightmares of fear and madness that seemed to have ridden him up out of the black deeps. He shoved the great blocking stone back into place, and picking up the cloak he had left at the mouth of the tomb, he wrapped it about the Black Stone and hurried away, a strong revulsion and loathing shaking his soul and lending wings to his strides.

A gray silence brooded over the land. It was desolate as the blind side of the moon, yet Bran felt the potentialities of life – under his feet, in the brown earth – sleeping, but how soon to waken, and in what horrific fashion?

He came through the tall masking reeds to the still deep men called Dagon's Mere. No slightest ripple ruffled the cold blue water to give evidence of the grisly monster legend said dwelt beneath. Bran closely scanned the breathless landscape. He saw no hint of life, human or unhuman. He sought the instincts of his savage soul to know if any unseen eyes fixed their lethal gaze upon him, and found no response. He was alone as if he were the last man alive on earth.

Swiftly he unwrapped the Black Stone, and as it lay in his hands like a solid sullen block of darkness, he did not seek to learn the secret of its material nor scan the cryptic characters carved thereon. Weighing it in his hands and calculating the distance, he flung it far out, so that it fell almost exactly in the middle of the lake. A sullen splash and the waters closed over it. There was a moment of shimmering flashes on the bosom of the lake; then the blue surface stretched placid and unrippled again.

Chapter 5

The were-woman turned swiftly as Bran approached her door. Her slant eyes widened.

"You! And alive! And sane!"

"I have been into Hell and I have returned," he growled. "What is more, I have that which I sought."

"The Black Stone?" she cried. "You really dared steal it? Where is it?"

"No matter; but last night my stallion screamed in his stall and I heard something crunch beneath his thundering hoofs which was not the wall of the stable – and there was blood on his hoofs when I came to see, and blood on the floor of the stall. And I have heard stealthy sounds in the night, and noises beneath my dirt floor, as if worms burrowed deep in the earth. They know I have stolen their Stone. Have you betrayed me?"

She shook her head.

"I keep your secret; they do not need my word to know you. The farther they have retreated from the world of men, the greater have grown their powers in other uncanny ways. Some dawn your hut will stand empty and if men dare investigate they will find nothing – except crumbling bits of earth on the dirt floor."

Bran smiled terribly.

"I have not planned and toiled thus far to fall prey to the talons of vermin. If They strike me down in the night, They will never know what became of their idol – or whatever it be to Them. I would speak with Them."

"Dare you come with me and meet them in the night?" she asked.

"Thunder of all gods!" he snarled. "Who are you to ask me if I dare? Lead me to Them and let me bargain for a vengeance this night. The hour of retribution draws nigh. This day I saw silvered helmets and bright shields gleam across the fens – the new commander has arrived at the Tower of Trajan and Caius Camillus has marched to the Wall."

That night the king went across the dark desolation of the moors with the silent were-woman. The night was thick and still as if the land lay in ancient slumber. The stars blinked vaguely, mere points of red struggling through the unbreathing gloom. Their gleam was dimmer than the glitter in the eyes of the woman who glided beside the king. Strange thoughts shook Bran, vague, titanic, primeval. Tonight ancestral linkings with these slumbering fens stirred in his soul and troubled him with the phantasmal, eon-veiled shapes of monstrous dreams. The vast age of his race was borne upon him; where now he walked an outlaw and an alien, dark-eyed kings in whose mold he was cast had reigned in old times. The Celtic and Roman invaders were as strangers to this ancient isle beside his people. Yet his race likewise had been invaders, and there was an older race than his – a race whose beginnings lay lost and hidden back beyond the dark oblivion of antiquity.

Ahead of them loomed a low range of hills, which formed the easternmost extremity of those straying chains which far away climbed at last to the mountains of Wales. The woman led the way up what might have been a sheep-path, and halted before a wide black gaping cave.

"A door to those you seek, oh king!" her laughter rang hateful in the gloom. "Dare ye enter?"

His fingers closed in her tangled locks and he shook her viciously.

"Ask me but once more if I dare," he grated, "and your head and shoulders part company! Lead on."

Her laughter was like sweet deadly venom. They passed into the cave and Bran struck flint and steel. The flicker of the tinder showed him a wide dusty cavern, on the roof of which hung clusters of bats. Lighting a torch, he lifted it and scanned the shadowy recesses, seeing nothing but dust and emptiness.

"Where are They?" he growled.

She beckoned him to the back of the cave and leaned against the rough wall, as if casually. But the king's keen eyes caught the motion of her hand pressing hard against a projecting ledge. He recoiled as a round black well gaped suddenly at his feet. Again her laughter slashed him like a keen silver knife. He held the torch to the opening and again saw small worn steps leading down.

"They do not need those steps," said Atla. "Once they did, before your people drove them into the darkness. But you will need them."

She thrust the torch into a niche above the well; it shed a faint red light into the darkness below. She gestured into the well and Bran loosened his sword and stepped into the shaft. As he went down into the mystery of the darkness, the light was blotted out above him, and he thought for an instant Atla had covered the opening again. Then he realized that she was descending after him.

The descent was not a long one. Abruptly Bran felt his feet on a solid floor. Atla swung down beside him and stood in the dim circle of light that drifted down the shaft. Bran could not see the limits of the place into which he had come.

"Many caves in these hills," said Atla, her voice sounding small and strangely brittle in the vastness, "are but doors to greater caves which lie beneath, even as a man's words and deeds are but small indications of the dark caverns of murky thought lying behind and beneath."

And now Bran was aware of movement in the gloom. The darkness was filled with stealthy noises not like those made by any human foot. Abruptly sparks began to flash and float in the blackness, like flickering fireflies. Closer they came until they girdled him in a wide half-moon. And beyond the ring gleamed other sparks, a solid sea of them, fading away in the gloom until the farthest were mere tiny pin-points of light. And Bran knew they were the slanted eyes of the beings who had come upon him in such numbers that his brain reeled at the contemplation – and at the vastness of the cavern.

Now that he faced his ancient foes, Bran knew no fear. He felt the waves of terrible menace emanating from them, the grisly hate, the inhuman threat to body, mind and soul. More than a member of a less ancient race, he realized the horror of his position, but he did not fear, though he confronted the ultimate Horror of the dreams and legends of his race. His blood raced fiercely but it was with the hot excitement of the hazard, not the drive of terror.

"They know you have the Stone, oh king," said Atla, and though he knew she feared, though he felt her physical efforts to control her trembling limbs, there was no quiver of fright in her voice. "You are in deadly peril; they know your breed of old – oh, they remember the days when their ancestors were men! I can not save you; both of us will die as no human has died for ten centuries. Speak to them, if you will; they can understand your speech, though you may not understand theirs. But it will avail not – you are human – and a Pict."

Bran laughed and the closing ring of fire shrank back at the savagery in his laughter. Drawing his sword with a soul-chilling rasp of steel, he set his back against what he hoped was a solid stone wall. Facing the glittering eyes with his sword gripped in his right hand and his dirk in his left, he laughed as a blood-hungry wolf snarls.

"Aye," he growled, "I am a Pict, a son of those warriors who drove your brutish ancestors before them like chaff before the storm! – who flooded the land with your blood and heaped high your skulls for a sacrifice to the Moon-Woman! You who fled of old before my race, dare ye now snarl at your master? Roll on me like a flood now, if ye dare! Before your viper fangs drink my life I will reap your multitudes like ripened barley – of your severed heads will I build a tower and of your mangled corpses will I rear up a wall! Dogs of the dark, vermin of Hell, worms of the earth, rush in and try my steel! When Death finds me in this dark cavern, your living will howl for the scores of your dead and your Black Stone will be lost to you forever – for only I know where it is hidden and not all the tortures of all the Hells can wring the secret from my lips!"

Then followed a tense silence; Bran faced the fire-lit darkness, tensed like a wolf at bay, waiting the charge; at his side the woman cowered, her eyes ablaze. Then from the silent ring that hovered beyond the dim torchlight rose a vague abhorrent murmur. Bran, prepared as he was for anything, started. Gods, was that the speech of creatures which had once been called men?

Atla straightened, listening intently. From her lips came the same hideous soft sibilances, and Bran, though he had already known the grisly secret of her being, knew that never again could he touch her save with soul-shaken loathing.

She turned to him, a strange smile curving her red lips dimly in the ghostly light.

"They fear you, oh king! By the black secrets of R'lyeh, who are you that Hell itself quails before you? Not your steel, but the stark ferocity of your soul has driven unused fear into their strange minds. They will buy back the Black Stone at any price."

"Good," Bran sheathed his weapons. "They shall promise not to molest you because of your aid of me. And," his voice hummed like the purr of a hunting tiger, "they shall deliver into my hands Titus Sulla, governor of Eboracum, now commanding the Tower of Trajan. This They can do – how, I know not. But I know that in the old days, when my people warred with these Children of the Night, babes disappeared from guarded huts and none saw the stealers come or go. Do They understand?"

Again rose the low frightful sounds and Bran, who feared not their wrath, shuddered at their voices.

"They understand," said Atla. "Bring the Black Stone to Dagon's Ring tomorrow night when the earth is veiled with the blackness that foreruns the dawn. Lay the Stone on the altar. There They will bring Titus Sulla to you. Trust Them; They have not interfered in human affairs for many centuries, but They will keep their word."

Bran nodded and turning, climbed up the stair with Atla close behind him. At the top he turned and looked down once more. As far as he could see floated a glittering ocean of slanted yellow eyes upturned. But the owners of those eyes kept carefully beyond the dim circle of torchlight and of their bodies he could see nothing. Their low hissing speech floated up to him and he shuddered as his imagination visualized, not a throng of biped creatures, but a swarming, swaying myriad of serpents, gazing up at him with their glittering unwinking eyes.

He swung into the upper cave and Atla thrust the blocking stone back in place. It fitted into the entrance of the well with uncanny precision; Bran was unable to discern any crack in the apparently solid floor of the cavern. Atla made a motion to extinguish the torch, but the king stayed her.

"Keep it so until we are out of the cave," he grunted. "We might tread on an adder in the dark."

Atla's sweetly hateful laughter rose maddeningly in the flickering gloom.

Chapter 6

It was not long before sunset when Bran came again to the reed-grown marge of Dagon's Mere. Casting cloak and sword-belt on the ground, he stripped himself of his short leathern breeches. Then gripping his naked dirk in his teeth, he went into the water with the smooth ease of a diving seal. Swimming strongly, he gained the center of the small lake, and turning, drove himself downward.

The mere was deeper than he had thought. It seemed he would never reach the bottom, and when he did, his groping hands failed to find what he sought. A roaring in his ears warned him and he swam to the surface.

Gulping deep of the refreshing air, he dived again, and again his quest was fruitless. A third time he sought the depth, and this time his groping hands met a familiar object in the silt of the bottom. Grasping it, he swam up to the surface.

The Stone was not particularly bulky, but it was heavy. He swam leisurely, and suddenly was aware of a curious stir in the waters about him which was not caused by his own exertions. Thrusting his face below the surface, he tried to pierce the blue depths with his eyes and thought to see a dim gigantic shadow hovering there.

He swam faster, not frightened, but wary. His feet struck the shallows and he waded up on the shelving shore. Looking back he saw the waters swirl and subside. He shook his head, swearing. He had discounted the ancient legend which made Dagon's Mere the lair of a nameless water-monster, but now he had a feeling as if his escape had been narrow. The time-worn myths of the ancient land were taking form and coming to life before his eyes. What primeval shape lurked below the surface of that treacherous mere, Bran could not guess, but he felt that the fenmen had good reason for shunning the spot, after all.

Bran donned his garments, mounted the black stallion and rode across the fens in the desolate crimson of the sunset's afterglow, with the Black Stone wrapped in his cloak. He rode, not to his hut, but to the west, in the direction of the Tower of Trajan and the Ring of Dagon. As he covered the miles that lay between, the red stars winked out. Midnight passed him in the moonless night and still Bran rode on. His heart was hot for his meeting with Titus Sulla. Atla had gloated over the anticipation of watching the Roman writhe under torture, but no such thought was in the Pict's mind. The governor should have his chance with weapons – with Bran's own sword he should face the Pictish king's dirk, and live or die according to his prowess. And though Sulla was famed throughout the provinces as a swordsman, Bran felt no doubt as to the outcome.

Dagon's Ring lay some distance from the Tower – a sullen circle of tall gaunt stones planted upright, with a rough-hewn stone altar in the center. The Romans looked on these menhirs with aversion; they thought the Druids had reared them; but the Celts supposed Bran's people, the Picts, had planted them – and Bran well knew what hands reared those grim monoliths in lost ages, though for what reasons, he but dimly guessed.

The king did not ride straight to the Ring. He was consumed with curiosity as to how his grim allies intended carrying out their promise. That They could snatch Titus Sulla from the very midst of his men, he felt sure, and he believed he knew how They would do it. He felt the gnawings of a strange misgiving, as if he had tampered with powers of unknown breadth and depth, and had loosed forces which he could not control. Each time he remembered that reptilian murmur, those slanted eyes of the night before, a cold breath passed over him. They had been abhorrent enough when his people drove Them into the caverns under the hills, ages ago; what had long centuries of retrogression made of them? In their nighted, subterranean life, had They retained any of the attributes of humanity at all?

Some instinct prompted him to ride toward the Tower. He knew he was near; but for the thick darkness he could have plainly seen its stark outline tusking the horizon. Even now he should be able to make it out dimly. An obscure, shuddersome premonition shook him and he spurred the stallion into swift canter.

And suddenly Bran staggered in his saddle as from a physical impact, so stunning was the surprize of what met his gaze. The impregnable Tower of Trajan was no more! Bran's astounded gaze rested on a gigantic pile of ruins – of shattered stone and crumbled granite, from which jutted the jagged and splintered ends of broken beams. At one corner of the tumbled heap one tower rose out of the waste of crumpled masonry, and it leaned drunkenly as if its foundations had been half-cut away.

Bran dismounted and walked forward, dazed by bewilderment. The moat was filled in places by fallen stones and broken pieces of mortared wall. He crossed over and came among the ruins. Where, he knew, only a few hours before the flags had resounded to the martial tramp of iron-clad feet, and the walls had echoed to the clang of shields and the blast of the loud-throated trumpets, a horrific silence reigned.

Almost under Bran's feet, a broken shape writhed and groaned. The king bent down to the legionary who lay in a sticky red pool of his own blood. A single glance showed the Pict that the man, horribly crushed and shattered, was dying.

Lifting the bloody head, Bran placed his flask to the pulped lips and the Roman instinctively drank deep, gulping through splintered teeth. In the dim starlight Bran saw his glazed eyes roll.

"The walls fell," muttered the dying man. "They crashed down like the skies falling on the day of doom. Ah Jove, the skies rained shards of granite and hailstones of marble!"

"I have felt no earthquake shock," Bran scowled, puzzled.

"It was no earthquake," muttered the Roman. "Before last dawn it began, the faint dim scratching and clawing far below the earth. We of the guard heard it – like rats burrowing, or like worms hollowing out the earth. Titus laughed at us, but all day long we heard it. Then at midnight the Tower quivered and seemed to settle – as if the foundations were being dug away–"

A shudder shook Bran Mak Morn. The worms of the earth! Thousands of vermin digging like moles far below the castle, burrowing away the foundations – gods, the land must be honeycombed with tunnels and caverns – these creatures were even less human than he had thought – what ghastly shapes of darkness had he invoked to his aid?

"What of Titus Sulla?" he asked, again holding the flask to the legionary's lips; in that moment the dying Roman seemed to him almost like a brother.

"Even as the Tower shuddered we heard a fearful scream from the governor's chamber," muttered the soldier. "We rushed there – as we broke down the door we heard his shrieks – they seemed to recede – into the bowels of the earth! We rushed in; the chamber was empty. His bloodstained sword lay on the floor; in the stone flags of the floor a black hole gaped. Then – the – towers – reeled – the – roof – broke; – through – a – storm – of – crashing – walls – I – crawled–"

A strong convulsion shook the broken figure.

"Lay me down, friend," whispered the Roman. "I die."

He had ceased to breathe before Bran could comply. The Pict rose, mechanically cleansing his hands. He hastened from the spot, and as he galloped over the darkened fens, the weight of the accursed Black Stone under his cloak was as the weight of a foul nightmare on a mortal breast.

As he approached the Ring, he saw an eerie glow within, so that the gaunt stones stood etched like the ribs of a skeleton in which a witch-fire burns. The stallion snorted and reared as Bran tied him to one of the menhirs. Carrying the Stone he strode into the grisly circle and saw Atla standing beside the altar, one hand on her hip, her sinuous body swaying in a serpentine manner. The altar glowed all over with ghastly light and Bran knew someone, probably Atla, had rubbed it with phosphorus from some dank swamp or quagmire.

He strode forward and whipping his cloak from about the Stone, flung the accursed thing on to the altar.

"I have fulfilled my part of the contract," he growled.

"And They, theirs," she retorted. "Look! – They come!"

He wheeled, his hand instinctively dropping to his sword. Outside the Ring the great stallion screamed savagely and reared against his tether. The night wind moaned through the waving grass and an abhorrent soft hissing mingled with it. Between the menhirs flowed a dark tide of shadows, unstable and chaotic. The Ring filled with glittering eyes which hovered beyond the dim illusive circle of illumination cast by the phosphorescent altar. Somewhere in the darkness a human voice tittered and gibbered idiotically. Bran stiffened, the shadows of a horror clawing at his soul.

He strained his eyes, trying to make out the shapes of those who ringed him. But he glimpsed only billowing masses of shadow which heaved and writhed and squirmed with almost fluid consistency.

"Let them make good their bargain!" he exclaimed angrily.

"Then see, oh king!" cried Atla in a voice of piercing mockery.

There was a stir, a seething in the writhing shadows, and from the darkness crept, like a four-legged animal, a human shape that fell down and groveled at Bran's feet and writhed and mowed, and lifting a death's-head, howled like a dying dog. In the ghastly light, Bran, soul-shaken, saw the blank glassy eyes, the bloodless features, the loose, writhing, froth-covered lips of sheer lunacy – gods, was this Titus Sulla, the proud lord of life and death in Eboracum's proud city?

Bran bared his sword.

"I had thought to give this stroke in vengeance," he said somberly. "I give it in mercy – Vale Cosar!"

The steel flashed in the eerie light and Sulla's head rolled to the foot of the glowing altar, where it lay staring up at the shadowed sky.

"They harmed him not!" Atla's hateful laugh slashed the sick silence. "It was what he saw and came to know that broke his brain! Like all his heavy-footed race, he knew nothing of the secrets of this ancient land. This night he has been dragged through the deepest pits of Hell, where even you might have blenched!"

"Well for the Romans that they know not the secrets of this accursed land!" Bran roared, maddened, "with its monster-haunted meres, its foul witch-women, and its lost caverns and subterranean realms where spawn in the darkness shapes of Hell!"

"Are they more foul than a mortal who seeks their aid?" cried Atla with a shriek of fearful mirth. "Give them their Black Stone!"

A cataclysmic loathing shook Bran's soul with red fury.

"Aye, take your cursed Stone!" he roared, snatching it from the altar and dashing it among the shadows with such savagery that bones snapped under its impact. A hurried babel of grisly tongues rose and the shadows heaved in turmoil. One segment of the mass detached itself for an instant and Bran cried out in fierce revulsion, though he caught only a fleeting glimpse of the thing, had only a brief impression of a broad strangely flattened head, pendulous writhing lips that bared curved pointed fangs, and a hideously misshapen, dwarfish body that seemed – mottled – all set off by those unwinking reptilian eyes. Gods! – the myths had prepared him for horror in human aspect, horror induced by bestial visage and stunted deformity – but this was the horror of nightmare and the night.

"Go back to Hell and take your idol with you!" he yelled, brandishing his clenched fists to the skies, as the thick shadows receded, flowing back and away from him like the foul waters of some black flood. "Your ancestors were men, though strange and monstrous – but gods, ye have become in ghastly fact what my people called ye in scorn! Worms of the earth, back into your holes and burrows! Ye foul the air and leave on the clean earth the slime of the serpents ye have become! Gonar was right – there are shapes too foul to use even against Rome!"

He sprang from the Ring as a man flees the touch of a coiling snake, and tore the stallion free. At his elbow Atla was shrieking with fearful laughter, all human attributes dropped from her like a cloak in the night.

"King of Pictland!" she cried, "King of fools! Do you blench at so small a thing? Stay and let me show you real fruits of the pits! Ha! ha! ha! Run, fool, run! But you are stained with the taint – you have called them forth and they will remember! And in their own time they will come to you again!"

He yelled a wordless curse and struck her savagely in the mouth with his open hand. She staggered, blood starting from her lips, but her fiendish laughter only rose higher.

Bran leaped into the saddle, wild for the clean heather and the cold blue hills of the north where he could plunge his sword into clean slaughter and his sickened soul into the red maelstrom of battle, and forget the horror which lurked below the fens of the west. He gave the frantic stallion the rein, and rode through the night like a hunted ghost, until the hellish laughter of the howling were-woman died out in the darkness behind.

The Lost Race

CORORUC glanced about him and hastened his pace. He was no coward, but he did not like the place. Tall trees rose all about, their sullen branches shutting out the sunlight. The dim trail led in and out among them, sometimes skirting the edge of a ravine, where Cororuc could gaze down at the treetops beneath. Occasionally, through a rift in the forest, he could see away to the forbidding hills that hinted of the ranges much farther to the west, that were the mountains of Cornwall.

In those mountains the bandit chief, Buruc the Cruel, was supposed to lurk, to descend upon such victims as might pass that way. Cororuc shifted his grip on his spear and quickened his step. His haste was due not only to the menace of the outlaws, but also to the fact that he wished once more to be in his native land. He had been on a secret mission to the wild Cornish tribesmen; and though he had been more or less successful, he was impatient to be out of their inhospitable country. It had been a long, wearisome trip, and he still had nearly the whole of Britain to traverse. He threw a glance of aversion about him. He longed for the pleasant woodlands, with scampering deer, and chirping birds, to which he was used. He longed for the tall white cliff, where the blue sea lapped merrily. The forest through which he was passing seemed uninhabited. There were no birds, no animals; nor had he seen a sign of human habitation.

His comrades still lingered at the savage court of the Cornish king, enjoying his crude hospitality, in no hurry to be away. But Cororuc was not content. So he had left them to follow at their leisure and had set out alone.

Rather a fine figure of a man was Cororuc. Some six feet in height, strongly though leanly built, he was, with gray eyes, a pure Briton but not a pure Celt, his long yellow hair revealing, in him as in all his race, a trace of Belgae.

He was clad in skillfully dressed deerskin, for the Celts had not yet perfected the coarse cloth which they made, and most of the race preferred the hides of deer.

He was armed with a long bow of yew wood, made with no especial skill but an efficient weapon; a long bronze broadsword, with a buckskin sheath; a long bronze dagger and a small, round shield, rimmed with a band of bronze and covered with tough buffalo hide. A crude bronze helmet was on his head. Faint devices were painted in woad on his arms and cheeks.

His beardless face was of the highest type of Briton, clear, straightforward, the shrewd, practical determination of the Nordic mingling with the reckless courage and dreamy artistry of the Celt.

So Cororuc trod the forest path, warily, ready to flee or fight, but preferring to do neither just then.

The trail led away from the ravine, disappearing around a great tree. And from the other side of the tree, Cororuc heard sounds of conflict. Gliding warily forward, and wondering whether he should see some of the elves and dwarfs that were reputed to haunt those woodlands, he peered around the great tree.

A few feet from him he saw a strange tableau. Backed against another tree stood a large wolf, at bay, blood trickling from gashes about his shoulder; while before him, crouching for a spring, the warrior saw a great panther. Cororuc wondered at the cause of the battle. Not often the lords of the forest met in warfare. And he was puzzled by the snarls of the great cat. Savage, blood-lusting, yet they held a strange note of fear; and the beast seemed hesitant to spring in.

Just why Cororuc chose to take the part of the wolf, he himself could not have said. Doubtless it was just the reckless chivalry of the Celt in him, an admiration for the dauntless attitude of the wolf against his far more powerful foe. Be that as it may, Cororuc, characteristically forgetting his bow and taking the more reckless course, drew his sword and leaped in front of the panther. But he had no chance to use it. The panther, whose nerve appeared to be already somewhat shaken, uttered a startled screech and disappeared among the trees so quickly that Cororuc wondered if he had really seen a panther. He turned to the wolf, wondering if it would leap upon him. It was watching him, half crouching; slowly it stepped away from the tree, and still watching him, backed away a few yards, then turned and made off with a strange shambling gait. As the warrior watched it vanish into the forest, an uncanny feeling came over him; he had seen many wolves, he had hunted them and had been hunted by them, but he had never seen such a wolf before.

He hesitated and then walked warily after the wolf, following the tracks that were plainly defined in the soft loam. He did not hasten, being merely content to follow the tracks. After a short distance, he stopped short, the hairs on his neck seeming to bristle. *Only the tracks of the hind feet showed: the wolf was walking erect.*

He glanced about him. There was no sound; the forest was silent. He felt an impulse to turn and put as much territory between him and the mystery as possible, but his Celtic curiosity would not allow it. He followed the trail. And then it ceased altogether. Beneath a great tree the tracks vanished. Cororuc felt the cold sweat on his forehead. What kind of place was that forest? Was he being led astray and eluded by some inhuman, supernatural monster of the woodlands, who sought to ensnare him? And Cororuc backed away, his sword lifted, his courage not allowing him to run, but greatly desiring to do so. And so he came again to the tree where he had first seen the wolf. The trail he had followed led away from it in another direction and Cororuc took it up, almost running in his haste to get out of the vicinity of a wolf who walked on two legs and then vanished in the air.

The trail wound about more tediously than ever, appearing and disappearing within a dozen feet, but it was well for Cororuc that it did, for thus he heard the voices of the men coming up the path before they saw him. He took to a tall tree that branched over the trail, lying close to the great bole, along a wide-flung branch.

Three men were coming down the forest path.

One was a big, burly fellow, vastly over six feet in height, with a long red beard and a great mop of red hair. In contrast, his eyes were a beady black. He was dressed in deerskins, and armed with a great sword.

Of the two others, one was a lanky, villainous-looking scoundrel, with only one eye, and the other was a small, wizened man, who squinted hideously with both beady eyes.

Cororuc knew them, by descriptions the Cornishmen had made between curses, and it was in his excitement to get a better view of the most villainous murderer in Britain that he slipped from the tree branch and plunged to the ground directly between them.

He was up on the instant, his sword out. He could expect no mercy; for he knew that the red-haired man was Buruc the Cruel, the scourge of Cornwall.

The bandit chief bellowed a foul curse and whipped out his great sword. He avoided the Briton's furious thrust by a swift backward leap and then the battle was on. Buruc rushed the warrior from the front, striving to beat him down by sheer weight; while the lanky, one-eyed villain slipped around, trying to get behind him. The smaller man had retreated to the edge of the forest. The fine art of the fence was unknown to those early swordsmen. It was hack, slash, stab, the full weight of the arm behind each blow. The terrific blows crashing on his shield beat Cororuc to the ground, and the lanky, one-eyed villain rushed in to finish him. Cororuc spun about without rising, cut the bandit's legs from under him and stabbed him as he fell, then threw himself to one side and to his feet, in time to avoid Buruc's sword. Again, driving his shield up to catch the bandit's sword in midair, he deflected it and whirled his own with all his power. Buruc's head flew from his shoulders.

Then Cororuc, turning, saw the wizened bandit scurry into the forest. He raced after him, but the fellow had disappeared among the trees. Knowing the uselessness of attempting to pursue him, Cororuc turned and raced down the trail. He did not know if there were more bandits in that direction, but he did know that if he expected to get out of the forest at all, he would have to do it swiftly. Without doubt the villain who had escaped would have all the other bandits out, and soon they would be beating the woodlands for him.

After running for some distance down the path and seeing no sign of any enemy, he stopped and climbed into the topmost branches of a tall tree that towered above its fellows.

On all sides he seemed surrounded by a leafy ocean. To the west he could see the hills he had avoided. To the north, far in the distance, other hills rose; to the south the forest ran, an unbroken sea. But to the east, far away, he could barely see the line that marked the thinning out of the forest into the fertile plains. Miles and miles away, he knew not how many, but it meant more pleasant travel, villages of men, people of his own race. He was surprized that he was able to see that far, but the tree in which he stood was a giant of its kind.

Before he started to descend, he glanced about nearer at hand. He could trace the faintly marked line of the trail he had been following, running away into the east; and could make out other trails leading into it, or away from it. Then a glint caught his eye. He fixed his gaze on a glade some distance down the trail and saw, presently, a party of men enter and vanish. Here and there, on every trail, he caught glances of the glint of accouterments, the waving of foliage. So the squinting villain had already roused the bandits. They were all around him; he was virtually surrounded.

A faintly heard burst of savage yells, from back up the trail, startled him. So, they had already thrown a cordon about the place of the fight and had found him gone. Had he not fled swiftly, he would have been caught. He was outside the cordon, but the bandits were all about him. Swiftly he slipped from the tree and glided into the forest.

Then began the most exciting hunt Cororuc had ever engaged in; for he was the hunted and men were the hunters. Gliding, slipping from bush to bush and from tree to tree, now running swiftly, now crouching in a covert, Cororuc fled, ever eastward, not daring to turn back lest he be driven farther back into the forest. At times he was forced to turn his course; in fact, he very seldom fled in a straight course, yet always he managed to work farther eastward.

Sometimes he crouched in bushes or lay along some leafy branch, and saw bandits pass so close to him that he could have touched them. Once or twice they sighted him and he fled, bounding over logs and bushes, darting in and out among the trees; and always he eluded them.

It was in one of those headlong flights that he noticed he had entered a defile of small hills, of which he had been unaware, and looking back over his shoulder, saw that his pursuers had halted, within full sight. Without pausing to ruminate on so strange a thing, he darted around a great boulder, felt a vine or something catch his foot, and was thrown headlong. Simultaneously, something struck the youth's head, knocking him senseless.

When Cororuc recovered his senses, he found that he was bound, hand and foot. He was being borne along, over rough ground. He looked about him. Men carried him on their shoulders, but such men as he had never seen before. Scarce above four feet stood the tallest, and they were small of build and very dark of complexion. Their eyes were black; and most of them went stooped forward, as if from a lifetime spent in crouching and hiding; peering furtively on all sides. They were armed with small bows, arrows, spears and daggers, all pointed, not with crudely worked bronze but with flint and obsidian, of the finest workmanship. They were dressed in finely dressed hides of rabbits and other small animals, and a kind of coarse cloth; and many were tattooed from head to foot in ocher and woad. There were perhaps twenty in all. What sort of men were they? Cororuc had never seen the like.

They were going down a ravine, on both sides of which steep cliffs rose. Presently they seemed to come to a blank wall, where the ravine appeared to come to an abrupt stop. Here, at a word from one who seemed to be in command, they set the Briton down, and seizing hold of a large boulder, drew it to one side. A small cavern was exposed, seeming to vanish away into the earth; then the strange men picked up the Briton and moved forward.

Cororuc's hair bristled at the thought of being borne into that forbidding-looking cave. What manner of men were they? In all Britain and Alba, in Cornwall or Ireland, Cororuc had never seen such men. Small dwarfish men, who dwelt in the earth. Cold sweat broke out on the youth's forehead. Surely they were the malevolent dwarfs of whom the Cornish people had spoken, who dwelt in their caverns by day, and by night sallied forth to steal and burn dwellings, even slaying if the opportunity arose! You will hear of them, even today, if you journey in Cornwall.

The men, or elves, if such they were, bore him into the cavern, others entering and drawing the boulder back into place. For a moment all was darkness, and then torches began to glow, away off. And at a shout they moved on. Other men of the caves came forward, with the torches.

Cororuc looked about him. The torches shed a vague glow over the scene. Sometimes one, sometimes another wall of the cave showed for an instant, and the Briton was vaguely aware that they were covered with paintings, crudely done, yet with a certain skill his own race could not equal. But always the roof remained unseen. Cororuc knew that the seemingly small cavern had merged into a cave of surprizing size. Through the vague light of the torches the strange people moved, came and went, silently, like shadows of the dim past.

He felt the cords of thongs that bound his feet loosened. He was lifted upright.

"Walk straight ahead," said a voice, speaking the language of his own race, and he felt a spear point touch the back of his neck.

And straight ahead he walked, feeling his sandals scrape on the stone floor of the cave, until they came to a place where the floor tilted upward. The pitch was steep and the stone was so slippery that Cororuc could not have climbed it alone. But his captors pushed him, and pulled him, and he saw that long, strong vines were strung from somewhere at the top.

Those the strange men seized, and bracing their feet against the slippery ascent, went up swiftly. When their feet found level surface again, the cave made a turn, and Cororuc blundered out into a fire-lit scene that made him gasp.

The cave debouched into a cavern so vast as to be almost incredible. The mighty walls swept up into a great arched roof that vanished in the darkness. A level floor lay between, and through it flowed a river; an underground river. From under one wall it flowed to vanish silently under the other. An arched stone bridge, seemingly of natural make, spanned the current.

All around the walls of the great cavern, which was roughly circular, were smaller caves, and before each glowed a fire. Higher up were other caves, regularly arranged, tier on tier. Surely human men could not have built such a city.

In and out among the caves, on the level floor of the main cavern, people were going about what seemed daily tasks. Men were talking together and mending weapons, some were fishing from the river; women were replenishing fires, preparing garments; and altogether it might have been any other village in Britain, to judge from their occupations. But it all struck Cororuc as extremely unreal; the strange place, the small, silent people, going about their tasks, the river flowing silently through it all.

Then they became aware of the prisoner and flocked about him. There was none of the shouting, abuse and indignities, such as savages usually heap on their captives, as the small men drew about Cororuc, silently eying him with malevolent, wolfish stares. The warrior shuddered, in spite of himself.

But his captors pushed through the throng, driving the Briton before them. Close to the bank of the river, they stopped and drew away from around him.

Two great fires leaped and flickered in front of him and there was something between them. He focused his gaze and presently made out the object. A high stone seat, like a throne; and in it seated an aged man, with a long white beard, silent, motionless, but with black eyes that gleamed like a wolf's.

The ancient was clothed in some kind of a single, flowing garment. One claw-like hand rested on the seat near him, skinny, crooked fingers, with talons like a hawk's. The other hand was hidden among his garments.

The firelight danced and flickered; now the old man stood out clearly, his hooked, beak-like nose and long beard thrown into bold relief; now he seemed to recede until he was invisible to the gaze of the Briton, except for his glittering eyes.

"Speak, Briton!" The words came suddenly, strong, clear, without a hint of age. "Speak, what would ye say?"

Cororuc, taken aback, stammered and said, "Why, why – what manner people are you? Why have you taken me prisoner? Are you elves?"

"We are Picts," was the stern reply.

"Picts!" Cororuc had heard tales of those ancient people from the Gaelic Britons; some said that they still lurked in the hills of Siluria, but –

"I have fought Picts in Caledonia," the Briton protested; "they are short but massive and misshapen; not at all like you!"

"They are not true Picts," came the stern retort. "Look about you, Briton," with a wave of an arm, "you see the remnants of a vanishing race; a race that once ruled Britain from sea to sea."

The Briton stared, bewildered.

"Harken, Briton," the voice continued; "harken, barbarian, while I tell to you the tale of the lost race."

The firelight flickered and danced, throwing vague reflections on the towering walls and on the rushing, silent current.

The ancient's voice echoed through the mighty cavern.

"Our people came from the south. Over the islands, over the Inland Sea. Over the snow-topped mountains, where some remained, to slay any enemies who might follow. Down into the fertile plains we came. Over all the land we spread.

We became wealthy and prosperous. Then two kings arose in the land, and he who conquered, drove out the conquered. So many of us made boats and set sail for the far-off cliffs that gleamed white in the sunlight. We found a fair land with fertile plains. We found a race of red-haired barbarians, who dwelt in caves. Mighty giants, of great bodies and small minds.

"We built our huts of wattle. We tilled the soil. We cleared the forest. We drove the red-haired giants back into the forest. Farther we drove them back until at last they fled to the mountains of the west and the mountains of the north. We were rich. We were prosperous.

"Then," and his voice thrilled with rage and hate, until it seemed to reverberate through the cavern, "then the Celts came. From the isles of the west, in their rude coracles they came. In the west they landed, but they were not satisfied with the west. They marched eastward and seized the fertile plains. We fought. They were stronger. They were fierce fighters and they were armed with weapons of bronze, whereas we had only weapons of flint.

"We were driven out. They enslaved us. They drove us into the forest. Some of us fled into the mountains of the west. Many fled into the mountains of the north. There they mingled with the red-haired giants we drove out so long ago, and became a race of monstrous dwarfs, losing all the arts of peace and gaining only the ability to fight.

"But some of us swore that we would never leave the land we had fought for. But the Celts pressed us. There were many, and more came. So we took to caverns, to ravines, to caves. We, who had always dwelt in huts that let in much light, who had always tilled the soil, we learned to dwell like beasts, in caves where no sunlight ever entered. Caves we found, of which this is the greatest; caves we made.

"You, Briton," the voice became a shriek and a long arm was outstretched in accusation, "you and your race! You have made a free, prosperous nation into a race of earth-rats! We who never fled, who dwelt in the air and the sunlight close by the sea where traders came, we must flee like hunted beasts and burrow like moles! But at night! Ah, then for our vengeance! Then we slip from our hiding places, ravines and caves, with torch and dagger! Look, Briton!"

And following the gesture, Cororuc saw a rounded post of some kind of very hard wood, set in a niche in the stone floor, close to the bank. The floor about the niche was charred as if by old fires.

Cororuc stared, uncomprehending. Indeed, he understood little of what had passed. That these people were even human, he was not at all certain. He had heard so much of them as "little people." Tales of their doings, their hatred of the race of man, and their maliciousness flocked back to him. Little he knew that he was gazing on one of the mysteries of the ages. That the tales which the ancient Gaels told of the Picts, already warped, would become even more warped from age to age, to result in tales of elves, dwarfs, trolls and fairies, at first accepted and then rejected, entire, by the race of men, just as the Neanderthal monsters resulted in tales of goblins and ogres. But of that Cororuc neither knew nor cared, and the ancient was speaking again.

"There, there, Briton," exulted he, pointing to the post, "there you shall pay! A scant payment for the debt your race owes mine, but to the fullest of your extent."

The old man's exultation would have been fiendish, except for a certain high purpose in his face. He was sincere. He believed that he was only taking just vengeance; and he seemed like some great patriot for a mighty, lost cause.

"But I am a Briton!" stammered Cororuc. "It was not my people who drove your race into exile! They were Gaels, from Ireland. I am a Briton and my race came from Gallia only a hundred years ago. We conquered the Gaels and drove them into Erin, Wales and Caledonia, even as they drove your race."

"No matter!" The ancient chief was on his feet. "A Celt is a Celt. Briton, or Gael, it makes no difference. Had it not been Gael, it would have been Briton. Every Celt who falls into our hands must pay, be it warrior or woman, babe or king. Seize him and bind him to the post."

In an instant Cororuc was bound to the post, and he saw, with horror, the Picts piling firewood about his feet.

"And when you are sufficiently burned, Briton," said the ancient, "this dagger that has drunk the blood of a hundred Britons, shall quench its thirst in yours."

"But never have I harmed a Pict!" Cororuc gasped, struggling with his bonds.

"You pay, not for what you did, but for what your race has done," answered the ancient sternly. "Well do I remember the deeds of the Celts when first they landed on Britain – the shrieks of the slaughtered, the screams of ravished girls, the smokes of burning villages, the plundering."

Cororuc felt his short neck-hairs bristle. When first the Celts landed on Britain! That was over five hundred years ago!

And his Celtic curiosity would not let him keep still, even at the stake with the Picts preparing to light firewood piled about him.

"You could not remember that. That was ages ago."

The ancient looked at him somberly. "And I am age-old. In my youth I was a witch-finder, and an old woman witch cursed me as she writhed at the stake. She said I should live until the last child of the Pictish race had passed. That I should see the once mighty nation go down into oblivion and then – and only then – should I follow it. For she put upon me the curse of life everlasting."

Then his voice rose until it filled the cavern. "But the curse was nothing. Words can do no harm, can do nothing, to a man. I live. A hundred generations have I seen come and go, and yet another hundred. What is time? The sun rises and sets, and another day has passed into oblivion. Men watch the sun and set their lives by it. They league themselves on every hand with time. They count the minutes that race them into eternity. Man outlived the centuries ere he began to reckon time. Time is man-made. Eternity is the work of the gods. In this cavern there is no such thing as time. There are no stars, no sun. Without is time; within is eternity. We count not time. Nothing marks the speeding of the hours. The youths go forth. They see the sun, the stars. They reckon time. And they pass. I was a young man when I entered this cavern. I have never left it. As you reckon time, I may have dwelt here a thousand years; or an hour. When not banded by time, the soul, the mind, call it what you will, can conquer the body. And the wise men of the race, in my youth, knew more than the outer world will ever learn. When I feel that my body begins to weaken, I take the magic draft, that is known only to me, of all the world. It does not give immortality; that is the work of the mind alone; but it rebuilds the body. The race of Picts vanish; they fade like the snow on the mountain. And when the last is gone, this dagger shall free me from the world." Then in a swift change of tone, "Light the fagots!"

Cororuc's mind was fairly reeling. He did not in the least understand what he had just heard. He was positive that he was going mad; and what he saw the next minute assured him of it.

Through the throng came a wolf; and he knew that it was the wolf whom he had rescued from the panther close by the ravine in the forest!

Strange, how long ago and far away that seemed! Yes, it was the same wolf. That same strange, shambling gait. Then the thing stood erect and raised its front feet to its head. What nameless horror was that?

Then the wolf's head fell back, disclosing a man's face. The face of a Pict; one of the first "werewolves." The man stepped out of the wolfskin and strode forward, calling something. A Pict just starting to light the wood about the Briton's feet drew back the torch and hesitated.

The wolf-Pict stepped forward and began to speak to the chief, using Celtic, evidently for the prisoner's benefit. Cororuc was surprized to hear so many speak his language, not reflecting upon its comparative simplicity, and the ability of the Picts.

"What is this?" asked the Pict who had played wolf. "A man is to be burned who should not be!"

"How?" exclaimed the old man fiercely, clutching his long beard. "Who are you to go against a custom of age-old antiquity?"

"I met a panther," answered the other, "and this Briton risked his life to save mine. Shall a Pict show ingratitude?"

And as the ancient hesitated, evidently pulled one way by his fanatical lust for revenge, and the other by his equally fierce racial pride, the Pict burst into a wild flight of oration, carried on in his own language. At last the ancient chief nodded.

"A Pict ever paid his debts," said he with impressive grandeur. "Never a Pict forgets. Unbind him. No Celt shall ever say that a Pict showed ingratitude."

Cororuc was released, and as, like a man in a daze, he tried to stammer his thanks, the chief waved them aside.

"A Pict never forgets a foe, ever remembers a friendly deed," he replied.

"Come," murmured his Pictish friend, tugging at the Celt's arm.

He led the way into a cave leading away from the main cavern. As they went, Cororuc looked back, to see the ancient chief seated upon his stone throne, his eyes gleaming as he seemed to gaze back through the lost glories of the ages; on each hand the fires leaped and flickered. A figure of grandeur, the king of a lost race.

On and on Cororuc's guide led him. And at last they emerged and the Briton saw the starlit sky above him.

"In that way is a village of your tribesmen," said the Pict, pointing, "where you will find a welcome until you wish to take up your journey anew."

And he pressed gifts on the Celt; gifts of garments of cloth and finely worked deerskin, beaded belts, a fine horn bow with arrows skillfully tipped with obsidian. Gifts of food. His own weapons were returned to him.

"But an instant," said the Briton, as the Pict turned to go. "I followed your tracks in the forest. They vanished." There was a question in his voice.

The Pict laughed softly. "I leaped into the branches of the tree. Had you looked up, you would have seen me. If ever you wish a friend, you will ever find one in Berula, chief among the Alban Picts."

He turned and vanished. And Cororuc strode through the moonlight toward the Celtic village.

The Valley of the Worm

I WILL TELL YOU OF NIORD AND THE WORM. You have heard the tale before in many guises wherein the hero was named Tyr, or Perseus, or Siegfried, or Beowulf, or St George. But it was Niord who met the loathly demoniac thing that crawled hideously up from hell, and from which meeting sprang the cycle of hero-tales that revolves down the ages until the very substance of the truth is lost and passes into the limbo of all forgotten legends. I know whereof I speak, for I was Niord.

As I lie here awaiting death, which creeps slowly upon me like a blind slug, my dreams are filled with glittering visions and the pageantry of glory. It is not of the drab, disease-racked life of James Allison I dream, but all the gleaming figures of the mighty pageantry that have passed before, and shall come after; for I have faintly glimpsed, not merely the shapes that come after, as a man in a long parade glimpses, far ahead, the line of figures that precede him winding over a distant hill, etched shadow-like against the sky. I am one and all the pageantry of shapes and guises and masks which have been, are, and shall be the visible manifestations of that illusive, intangible, but vitally existent spirit now promenading under the brief and temporary name of James Allison.

Each man on earth, each woman, is part and all of a similar caravan of shapes and beings. But they cannot remember – their minds cannot bridge the brief, awful gulfs of blackness which he between those unstable shapes, and which the spirit, soul or ego, in spanning, shakes off its fleshy masks. I remember. Why I can remember is the strangest tale of all; but as I lie here with death's black wings slowly unfolding over me, all the dim folds of my previous lives are shaken out before my eyes, and I see myself in many forms and guises – braggart, swaggering, fearful, loving, foolish, all that men have been or will be.

I have been man in many lands and many conditions; yet – and here is another strange thing – my line of reincarnation runs straight down one unerring channel. I have never been any but a man of that restless race men once called Nordheimr and later Aryans, and today name by many names and designations. Their history is my history, from the first mewling wail of a hairless white ape cub in the wastes of the Arctic, to the death-cry of the last degenerate product of ultimate civilization, in some dim and unguessed future age.

My name has been Hialmar, Tyr, Bragi, Bran, Horsa, Eric and John. I strode red-handed through the deserted streets of Rome behind the yellow-maned Brennus; I wandered through the violated plantations with Alaric and his Goths when the flame of burning villas lit the land like day and an empire was gasping its last under our sandaled feet; I waded sword in hand through the foaming surf from Hengist's galley to lay the foundations of England in blood and pillage; when Leif the Lucky sighted the broad white beaches of an unguessed world, I stood beside him in the bows of the dragon-ship, my golden beard blowing in the wind; and when Godfrey of Bouillon led his Crusaders over the walls of Jerusalem, I was among them in steel cap and brigandine.

But it is of none of these things I would speak. I would take you back with me into an age beside which that of Brennus and Rome is as yesterday. I would take you back through, not merely centuries and millenniums, but epochs and dim ages unguessed by the wildest philosopher. Oh far, far and far will you fare into the nighted past before you win beyond the boundaries of my race, blue-eyed, yellow-haired, wanderers, slayers, lovers, mighty in rapine and wayfaring.

It is the adventure of Niord Worm's-bane of which I would speak – the rootstem of a whole cycle of hero tales which has not yet reached its end, the grisly underlying reality that lurks behind time-distorted myths of dragons, fiends and monsters.

Yet it is not alone with the mouth of Niord that I will speak. I am James Allison no less than I was Niord, and as I unfold the tale, I will interpret some of his thoughts and dreams and deeds from the mouth of the modern I, so that the saga of Niord shall not be a meaningless chaos to you. His blood is your blood, who are sons of Aryan; but wide misty gulfs of aeons lie horrifically between, and the deeds and dreams of Niord seem as alien to your deeds and dreams as the primordial and lion-haunted forest seems alien to the white-walled city street.

It was a strange world in which Niord lived and loved and fought, so long ago that even my aeon-spanning memory cannot recognize landmarks. Since then the surface of the earth has changed, not once but a score of times; continents have risen and sunk, seas have changed their beds and rivers their courses, glaciers have waxed and waned, and the very stars and constellations have altered and shifted.

It was so long ago that the cradle-land of my race was still in Nordheim. But the epic drifts of my people had already begun, and blue-eyed, yellow-maned tribes flowed eastward and southward and westward, on century-long treks that carried them around the world and left their bones and their traces in strange lands and wild waste places. On one of these drifts I grew from infancy to manhood. My knowledge of that northern homeland was dim memories, like half-remembered dreams, of blinding white snow plains and ice fields, of great fires roaring in the circle of hide tents, of yellow manes flying in great winds, and a sun setting in a lurid wallow of crimson clouds, blazing on trampled snow where still dark forms lay in pools that were redder than the sunset.

That last memory stands out clearer than the others. It was the field of Jötunheimr, I was told in later years, whereon had just been fought that terrible battle which was the Armageddon of the Æsir-folk, the subject of a cycle of hero-songs for long ages, and which still lives today in dim dreams of Ragnarök and Götterdämmerung. I looked on that battle as a mewling infant; so I must have lived about – but I will not name the age, for I would be called a madman, and historians and geologists alike would rise to refute me.

But my memories of Nordheim were few and dim, paled by memories of that long, long trek upon which I had spent my life. We had not kept to a straight course, but our trend had been for ever southward. Sometimes we had bided for a while in fertile upland valleys or rich river-traversed plains, but always we took up the trail again, and not always because of drought or famine. Often we left countries teeming with game and wild grain to push into wastelands. On our trail we moved endlessly, driven only by our restless whim, yet blindly following a cosmic law, the workings of which we never guessed, any more than the wild geese guess in their flights around the world. So at last we came into the Country of the Worm.

I will take up the tale at the time when we came into jungle-clad hills reeking with rot and teeming with spawning life, where the tom-toms of a savage people pulsed incessantly through the hot breathless night. These people came forth to dispute our way short, strongly built men, black-haired, painted, ferocious, but indisputably white men. We knew their breed of old. They were Picts, and of all alien races the fiercest. We had met their kind before in thick forests, and in upland valleys beside mountain lakes. But many moons had passed since those meetings.

I believe this particular tribe represented the easternmost drift of the race. They were the most primitive and ferocious of any I ever met. Already they were exhibiting hints of characteristics I have noted among black savages in jungle countries, though they had dwelled in these environs only a few generations. The abysmal jungle was engulfing them, was obliterating their pristine characteristics and shaping them in its own horrific mould. They were drifting into head-hunting, and cannibalism was but a step which I believe they must have taken before they became extinct. These things are natural adjuncts to the jungle; the Picts did not learn them from the black people, for then there were no blacks among those hills. In later years they came up from the south, and the Picts first enslaved and then were absorbed by them. But with that my saga of Niord is not concerned.

We came into that brutish hill country, with its squalling abysms of savagery and black primitiveness. We were a whole tribe marching on foot, old men, wolfish with their long beards and gaunt limbs, giant warriors in their prime, naked children running along the line of march, women with tousled yellow locks carrying babies which never cried – unless it were to scream from pure rage. I do not remember our numbers, except that there were some 500 fighting-men – and by fighting-men I mean all males, from the child just strong enough to lift a bow, to the oldest of the old men. In that madly ferocious age all were fighters. Our women fought, when brought to bay, like tigresses, and I have seen a babe, not yet old enough to stammer articulate words, twist its head and sink its tiny teeth in the foot that stamped out its life.

Oh, we were fighters! Let me speak of Niord. I am proud of him, the more when I consider the paltry crippled body of James Allison, the unstable mask I now wear. Niord was tall, with great shoulders, lean hips and mighty limbs. His muscles were long and swelling, denoting endurance and speed as well as strength. He could run all day without tiring, and he possessed a coordination that made his movements a blur of blinding speed. If I told you his full strength, you would brand me a liar. But there is no man on earth today strong enough to bend the bow Niord handled with ease. The longest arrow-flight on record is that of a Turkish archer who sent a shaft 482 yards. There was not a stripling in my tribe who could not have bettered that flight.

As we entered the jungle country we heard the tom-toms booming across the mysterious valleys that slumbered between the brutish hills, and in a broad, open plateau we met our enemies. I do not believe these Picts knew us, even by legends, or they had never rushed so openly to the onset, though they outnumbered us. But there was no attempt at ambush. They swarmed out of the trees, dancing and singing their war-songs, yelling their barbarous threats. Our heads should hang in their idol-hut and our yellow-haired women should bear their sons. Ho! ho! ho! By Ymir, it was Niord who laughed then, not James Allison. Just so we of the Æsir laughed to hear their threats – deep thunderous laughter from broad and mighty chests. Our trail was laid in blood and embers through many lands. We were the slayers and ravishers, striding sword in hand across the world, and that these folk threatened us woke our rugged humor.

We went to meet them, naked but for our wolfhides, swinging our bronze swords, and our singing was like rolling thunder in the hills. They sent their arrows among us, and we gave back their fire. They could not match us in archery. Our arrows hissed in blinding clouds among them, dropping them like autumn leaves, until they howled and frothed like mad dogs and changed to hand-grips. And we, mad with the fighting joy, dropped our bows and ran to meet them, as a lover runs to his love.

By Ymir, it was a battle to madden and make drunken with the slaughter and the fury. The Picts were as ferocious as we, but ours was the superior physique, the keener wit, the more highly developed fighting-brain. We won because we were a superior race, but it was no easy victory. Corpses littered the blood-soaked earth; but at last they broke, and we cut them down as they ran, to the very edge of the trees. I tell of that fight in a few bald words. I cannot paint the madness, the reek of sweat and blood, the panting, muscle-straining effort, the splintering of bones under mighty blows, the rending and hewing of quivering sentient flesh; above all the merciless abysmal savagery of the whole affair, in which there was neither rule nor order, each man fighting as he would or could. If I might do so, you would recoil in horror; even the modern I, cognizant of my close kinship with those times, stand aghast as I review that butchery. Mercy was yet unborn, save as some individual's whim, and rules of warfare were as yet undreamed of. It was an age in which each tribe and each human fought tooth and fang from birth to death, and neither gave nor expected mercy.

So we cut down the fleeing Picts, and our women came out on the field to brain the wounded enemies with stones, or cut their throats with copper knives. We did not torture. We were no more cruel than life demanded. The rule of life was ruthlessness, but there is more wanton cruelty today than ever we dreamed of. It was not wanton bloodthirstiness that made us butcher wounded and captive foes. It was because we knew our chances of survival increased with each enemy slain.

Yet there was occasionally a touch of individual mercy, and so it was in this fight. I had been occupied with a duel with an especially valiant enemy. His tousled thatch of black hair scarcely came above my chin, but he was a solid knot of steel-spring muscles, than which lightning scarcely moved faster. He had an iron sword and a hide-covered buckler. I had a knotty-headed bludgeon. That fight was one that glutted even my battle-lusting soul. I was bleeding from a score of flesh wounds before one of my terrible, lashing strokes smashed his shield like cardboard, and an instant later my bludgeon glanced from his unprotected head. Ymir! Even now I stop to laugh and marvel at the hardness of that Pict's skull. Men of that age were assuredly built on a rugged plan! That blow should have spattered his brains like water. It did lay his scalp open horribly, dashing him senseless to the earth, where I let him lie, supposing him to be dead, as I joined in the slaughter of the fleeing warriors.

When I returned reeking with sweat and blood, my club horridly clotted with blood and brains, I noticed that my antagonist was regaining consciousness, and that a naked tousle-headed girl was preparing to give him the finishing touch with a stone she could scarcely lift. A vagrant whim caused me to check the blow. I had enjoyed the fight, and I admired the adamantine quality of his skull.

We made camp a short distance away, burned our dead on a great pyre, and after looting the corpses of the enemy, we dragged them across the plateau and cast them down in a valley to make a feast for the hyenas, jackals and vultures which were already gathering. We kept close watch that night, but we were not attacked, though far away through the jungle we could make out the red gleam of fires, and could faintly hear, when the wind veered, the throb of tom-toms and demoniac screams and yells keenings for the slain or mere animal squallings of fury.

Nor did they attack us in the days that followed. We bandaged our captive's wounds and quickly learned his primitive tongue, which, however, was so different from ours that I cannot conceive of the two languages having ever had a common source.

His name was Grom, and he was a great hunter and fighter, he boasted. He talked freely and held no grudge, grinning broadly and showing tusk-like teeth, his beady eyes glittering from under the tangled black mane that fell over his low forehead. His limbs were almost ape-like in their thickness.

He was vastly interested in his captors, though he could never understand why he had been spared; to the end it remained an inexplicable mystery to him. The Picts obeyed the law of survival even more rigidly than did the Æsir. They were the more practical, as shown by their more settled habits. They never roamed as far or as blindly as we. Yet in every line we were the superior race.

Grom, impressed by our intelligence and fighting qualities, volunteered to go into the hills and make peace for us with his people. It was immaterial to us, but we let him go. Slavery had not yet been dreamed of.

So Grom went back to his people, and we forgot about him, except that I went a trifle more cautiously about my hunting, expecting him to be lying in wait to put an arrow through my back. Then one day we heard a rattle of tom-toms, and Grom appeared at the edge of the jungle, his face split in his gorilla grin, with the painted, skin-clad, feather-bedecked chiefs of the clans. Our ferocity had awed them, and our sparing of Grom further impressed them. They could not understand leniency; evidently we valued them too cheaply to bother about killing one when he was in our power.

So peace was made with much pow-wow, and sworn to with many strange oaths and rituals we swore only by Ymir, and an Æsir never broke that vow. But they swore by the elements, by the idol which sat in the fetish-hut where fires burned for ever and a withered crone slapped a leather-covered drum all night long, and by another being too terrible to be named.

Then we all sat around the fires and gnawed meat-bones, and drank a fiery concoction they brewed from wild grain, and the wonder is that the feast did not end in a general massacre; for that liquor had devils in it and made maggots writhe in our brains. But no harm came of our vast drunkenness, and thereafter we dwelled at peace with our barbarous neighbors. They taught us many things, and learned many more from us. But they taught us iron-workings, into which they had been forced by the lack of copper in those hills, and we quickly excelled them.

We went freely among their villages – mud-walled clusters of huts in hilltop clearings, overshadowed by giant trees – and we allowed them to come at will among our camps – straggling lines of hide tents on the plateau where the battle had been fought. Our young men cared not for their squat beady-eyed women, and our rangy clean-limbed girls with their tousled yellow heads were not drawn to the hairy-breasted savages. Familiarity over a period of years would have reduced the repulsion on either side, until the two races would have flowed together to form one hybrid people, but long before that time the Æsir rose and departed, vanishing into the mysterious hazes of the haunted south. But before that exodus there came to pass the horror of the Worm.

I hunted with Grom and he led me into brooding, uninhabited valleys and up into silence-haunted hills where no men had set foot before us. But there was one valley, off in the mazes of the south-west, into which he would not go. Stumps of shattered columns, relics of a forgotten civilization, stood among the trees on the valley floor. Grom showed them to me, as we stood on the cliffs that flanked the mysterious vale, but he would not go down into it, and he dissuaded me when I would have gone alone. He would not speak plainly of the danger that lurked there, but it was greater than that of serpent or tiger, or the trumpeting elephants which occasionally wandered up in devastating droves from the south.

Of all beasts, Grom told me in the gutturals of his tongue, the Picts feared only Satha, the great snake, and they shunned the jungle where he lived. But there was another thing they feared, and it was connected in some manner with the Valley of Broken Stones, as the Picts called the crumbling pillars. Long ago, when his ancestors had first come into the country, they had dared that grim vale, and a whole clan of them had perished, suddenly, horribly and unexplainably. At least Grom did not explain. The horror had come up out of the earth, somehow, and it was not good to talk of it, since it was believed that It might be summoned by speaking of It – whatever It was.

But Grom was ready to hunt with me anywhere else; for he was the greatest hunter among the Picts, and many and fearful were our adventures. Once I killed, with the iron sword I had forged with my own hands, that most terrible of all beasts – old saber-tooth, which men today call a tiger because he was more like a tiger than anything else. In reality he was almost as much like a bear in build, save for his unmistakably feline head. Saber-tooth was massive-limbed, with a low-hung, great, heavy body, and he vanished from the earth because he was too terrible a fighter, even for that grim age. As his muscles and ferocity grew, his brain dwindled until at last even the instinct of self-preservation vanished. Nature, who maintains her balance in such things, destroyed him because, had his super-fighting powers been allied with an intelligent brain, he would have destroyed all other forms of life on earth. He was a freak on the road of evolution organic development gone mad and run to fangs and talons, to slaughter and destruction.

I killed saber-tooth in a battle that would make a saga in itself, and for months afterwards I lay semi-delirious with ghastly wounds that made the toughest warriors shake their heads. The Picts said that never before had a man killed a saber-tooth single-handed. Yet I recovered, to the wonder of all.

While I lay at the doors of death there was a secession from the tribe. It was a peaceful secession, such as continually occurred and contributed greatly to the peopling of the world by yellow-haired tribes. Forty-five of the young men took themselves mates simultaneously and wandered off to found a clan of their own. There was no revolt; it was a racial custom which bore fruit in all the later ages, when tribes sprung from the same roots met, after centuries of separation, and cut one another's throats with joyous abandon. The tendency of the Aryan and the pre-Aryan was always towards disunity, clans splitting off the main stem, and scattering.

So these young men, led by one Bragi, my brother-in-arms, took their girls and venturing to the south-west, took up their abode in the Valley of Broken Stones. The Picts expostulated, hinting vaguely of a monstrous doom that haunted the vale, but the Æsir laughed. We had left our own demons and weirds in the icy wastes of the far blue north, and the devils of other races did not much impress us.

When my full strength was returned, and the grisly wounds were only scars, I girt on my weapons and strode over the plateau to visit Bragi's clan. Grom did not accompany me. He had not been in the Æsir camp for several days. But I knew the way. I remembered well the valley, from the cliffs of which I had looked down and seen the lake at the upper end, the trees thickening into forest at the lower extremity. The sides of the valley were high sheer cliffs, and a steep broad ridge at either end cut it off from the surrounding country. It was towards the lower or southwestern end that the valley floor was dotted thickly with ruined columns, some towering high among the trees, some fallen into heaps of lichen-clad stones. What race reared them none knew. But Grom had hinted fearsomely of a hairy, apish monstrosity dancing loathsomely under the moon to a demoniac piping that induced horror and madness.

I crossed the plateau whereon our camp was pitched, descended the slope, traversed a shallow vegetation-choked valley, climbed another slope, and plunged into the hills. A half-day's leisurely travel brought me to the ridge on the other side of which lay the valley of the pillars. For many miles I had seen no sign of human life. The settlements of the Picts all lay many miles to the east. I topped the ridge and looked down into the dreaming valley with its still blue lake, its brooding cliffs and its broken columns jutting among the trees. I looked for smoke. I saw none, but I saw vultures wheeling in the sky over a cluster of tents on the lake shore.

I came down the ridge warily and approached the silent camp. In it I halted, frozen with horror. I was not easily moved. I had seen death in many forms, and had fled from or taken part in red massacres that spilled blood like water and heaped the earth with corpses. But here I was confronted with an organic devastation that staggered and appalled me. Of Bragi's embryonic clan, not one remained alive, and not one corpse was whole. Some of the hide tents still stood erect. Others were mashed down and flattened out, as if crushed by some monstrous weight, so that at first I wondered if a drove of elephants had stampeded across the camp. But no elephants ever wrought such destruction as I saw strewn on the bloody ground. The camp was a shambles, littered with bits of flesh and fragments of bodies – hands, feet, heads, pieces of human debris. Weapons lay about, some of them stained with a greenish slime like that which spurts from a crushed caterpillar.

No human foe could have committed this ghastly atrocity. I looked at the lake, wondering if nameless amphibian monsters had crawled from the calm waters whose deep blue told of unfathomed depths. Then I saw a print left by the destroyer. It was a track such as a titanic worm might leave, yards broad, winding back down the valley. The grass lay flat where it ran, and bushes and small trees had been crushed down into the earth, all horribly smeared with blood and greenish slime.

With berserk fury in my soul I drew my sword and started to follow it, when a call attracted me. I wheeled, to see a stocky form approaching me from the ridge. It was Grom the Pict, and when I think of the courage it must have taken for him to have overcome all the instincts planted in him by traditional teachings and personal experience, I realize the full depths of his friendship for me.

Squatting on the lake shore, spear in his hands, his black eyes ever roving fearfully down the brooding tree-waving reaches of the valley, Grom told me of the horror that had come upon Bragi's clan under the moon. But first he told me of it, as his sires had told the tale to him.

Long ago the Picts had drifted down from the north-west on a long, long trek, finally reaching these jungle-covered hills, where, because they were weary, and because the game and fruit were plentiful and there were no hostile tribes, they halted and built their mud-walled villages.

Some of them, a whole clan of that numerous tribe, took up their abode in the Valley of the Broken Stones. They found the columns and a great ruined temple back in the trees, and in that temple there was no shrine or altar, but the mouth of a shaft that vanished deep into the black earth, and in which there were no steps such as a human being would make and use. They built their village in the valley, and in the night, under the moon, horror came upon them and left only broken walls and bits of slime-smeared flesh.

In those days the Picts feared nothing. The warriors of the other clans gathered and sang their war-songs and danced their war-dances, and followed a broad track of blood and slime to the shaft-mouth in the temple. They howled defiance and hurled down boulders which were never heard to strike bottom. Then began a thin demoniac piping, and up from the well pranced a hideous anthropomorphic figure dancing to the weird strains of a pipe it held in its monstrous hands. The horror of its aspect froze the fierce Picts with amazement, and close behind it a vast white bulk heaved up from the subterranean darkness. Out of the shaft came a slavering mad nightmare which arrows pierced but could not check, which swords carved but could not slay. It fell slobbering upon the warriors, crushing them to crimson pulp, tearing them to bits as an octopus might tear small fishes, sucking their blood from their mangled limbs and devouring them even as they screamed and struggled. The survivors fled, pursued to the very ridge, up which, apparently, the monster could not propel its quaking mountainous bulk.

After that they did not dare the silent valley. But the dead came to their shamans and old men in dreams and told them strange and terrible secrets. They spoke of an ancient, ancient race of semi-human beings which once inhabited that valley and reared those columns for their own weird inexplicable purposes. The white monster in the pits was their god, summoned up from the nighted abysses of mid-earth uncounted fathoms below the black mould by sorcery unknown to the sons of men. The hairy anthropomorphic being was its servant, created to serve the god, a formless elemental spirit drawn up from below and cased in flesh, organic but beyond the understanding of humanity. The Old Ones had long vanished into the limbo from whence they crawled in the black dawn of the universe, but their bestial god and his inhuman slave lived on. Yet both were organic after a fashion, and could be wounded, though no human weapon had been found potent enough to slay them.

Bragi and his clan had dwelled for weeks in the valley before the horror struck. Only the night before, Grom, hunting above the cliffs, and by that token daring greatly, had been paralyzed by a high-pitched demon piping, and then by a mad clamor of human screaming. Stretched face down in the dirt, hiding his head in a tangle of grass, he had not dared to move, even when the shrieks died away in the slobbering, repulsive sounds of a hideous feast. When dawn broke he had crept shuddering to the cliffs to look down into the valley, and the sight of the devastation, even when seen from afar, had driven him in yammering flight far into the hills. But it had occurred to him, finally, that he should warn the rest of the tribe, and returning, on his way to the camp on the plateau, he had seen me entering the valley.

So spoke Grom, while I sat and brooded darkly, my chin on my mighty fist. I cannot frame in modern words the clan feeling that in those days was a living vital part of every man and woman. In a world where talon and fang were lifted on every hand, and the hands of all men raised against an individual, except those of his own clan, tribal instinct was more than the phrase it is today. It was as much a part of a man as was his heart or his right hand. This was necessary, for only thus banded together in unbreakable groups could mankind have survived in the terrible environments of the primitive world. So now the personal grief I felt for Bragi and the clean-limbed young men and laughing white-skinned girls was drowned in a deeper sea of grief and fury that was cosmic in its depth and intensity. I sat grimly, while the Pict squatted anxiously beside me, his gaze roving from me to the menacing deeps of the valley where the accursed columns loomed like broken teeth of cackling hags among the waving leafy reaches.

I, Niord, was not one to use my brain over-much. I lived in a physical world, and there were the old men of the tribe to do my thinking. But I was one of a race destined to become dominant mentally as well as physically, and I was no mere muscular animal. So as I sat there, there came dimly and then clearly a thought to me that brought a short fierce laugh from my lips.

Rising, I bade Grom aid me, and we built a pyre on the lake shore of dried wood, the ridge-poles of the tents, and the broken shafts of spears. Then we collected the grisly fragments that had been parts of Bragi's band, and we laid them on the pile, and struck flint and steel to it.

The thick sad smoke crawled serpent-like into the sky, and, turning to Grom, I made him guide me to the jungle where lurked that scaly horror, Satha, the great serpent. Grom gaped at me; not the greatest hunters among the Picts sought out the mighty crawling one. But my will was like a wind that swept him along my course, and at last he led the way. We left the valley by the upper end, crossing the ridge, skirting the tall cliffs, and plunged into the fastnesses of the south, which was peopled only by the grim denizens of the jungle. Deep into the jungle we went, until we came to a low-lying expanse, dank and dark beneath the great creeper-festooned trees, where our feet sank deep into the spongy silt, carpeted by rotting vegetation, and slimy moisture oozed up beneath their pressure. This, Grom told me, was the realm haunted by Satha, the great serpent.

Let me speak of Satha. There is nothing like him on earth today, nor has there been for countless ages. Like the meat-eating dinosaur, like old saber-tooth, he was too terrible to exist. Even then he was a survival of a grimmer age when life and its forms were cruder and more hideous. There were not many of his kind then, though they may have existed in great numbers in the reeking ooze of the vast jungle-tangled swamps still further south. He was larger than any python of modern ages, and his fangs dripped with poison a thousand times more deadly than that of a king cobra.

He was never worshipped by the pure-blood Picts, though the blacks that came later deified him, and that adoration persisted in the hybrid race that sprang from the negroes and their white conquerors. But to other peoples he was the nadir of evil horror, and tales of him became twisted into demonology; so in later ages Satha became the veritable devil of the white races, and the Stygians first worshipped, and then, when they became Egyptians, abhorred him under the name of Set, the Old Serpent, while to the Semites he became Leviathan and Satan. He was terrible enough to be a god, for he was a crawling death. I had seen a bull elephant fall dead in his tracks from Satha's bite. I had seen him, had glimpsed him writhing his horrific way through the dense jungle, had seen him take his prey, but I had never hunted him. He was too grim, even for the slayer of old saber-tooth.

But now I hunted him, plunging further and further into the hot, breathless reek of his jungle, even when friendship for me could not drive Grom further. He urged me to paint my body and sing my death-song before I advanced further, but I pushed on unheeding.

In a natural runway that wound between the shouldering trees, I set a trap. I found a large tree, soft and spongy of fiber, but thick-boled and heavy, and I hacked through its base close to the ground with my great sword, directing its fall so that when it toppled, its top crashed into the branches of a smaller tree, leaving it leaning across the runway, one end resting on the earth, the other caught in the small tree. Then I cut away the branches on the underside, and cutting a slim, tough sapling I trimmed it and stuck it upright like a prop-pole under the leaning tree. Then, cutting away the tree which supported it, I left the great trunk poised precariously on the prop-pole, to which I fastened a long vine, as thick as my wrist.

Then I went alone through that primordial twilight jungle until an overpowering fetid odor assailed my nostrils, and from the rank vegetation in front of me Satha reared up his hideous head, swaying lethally from side to side, while his forked tongue jetted in and out, and his great yellow terrible eyes burned icily on me with all the evil wisdom of the black elder world that was when man was not. I backed away, feeling no fear, only an icy sensation along my spine, and Satha came sinuously after me, his shining 80-foot barrel rippling over the rotting vegetation in mesmeric silence. His wedge-shaped head was bigger than the head of the hugest stallion, his trunk was thicker than a man's body, and his scales shimmered with a thousand changing scintillations. I was to Satha as a mouse is to a king cobra, but I was fanged as no mouse ever was. Quick as I was, I knew I could not avoid the lightning stroke of that great triangular head; so I dared not let him come too close. Subtly I fled down the runway, and behind me the rush of the great supple body was like the sweep of wind through the grass.

He was not far behind me when I raced beneath the dead-fall, and as the great shining length glided under the trap, I gripped the vine with both hands and jerked desperately. With a crash the great trunk fell across Satha's scaly back, some 6 feet back of his wedge-shaped head.

I had hoped to break his spine but I do not think it did, for the great body coiled and knotted, the mighty tail lashed and thrashed, mowing down the bushes as if with a giant flail. At the instant of the fall, the huge head had whipped about and struck the tree with a terrific impact, the mighty fangs shearing through bark and wood like scimitars. Now, as if aware he fought an inanimate foe, Satha turned on me, standing out of his reach. The scaly neck writhed and arched, the mighty jaws gaped, disclosing fangs a foot in length, from which dripped venom that might have burned through solid stone.

I believe, what of his stupendous strength, that Satha would have writhed from under the trunk, but for a broken branch that had been driven deep into his side, holding him like a barb. The sound of his hissing filled the jungle and his eyes glared at me with such concentrated evil that I shook despite myself. Oh, he knew it was I who had trapped him! Now I came as close as I dared, and with a sudden powerful cast of my spear transfixed his neck just below the gaping jaws, nailing him to the tree-trunk. Then I dared greatly, for he was far from dead, and I knew he would in an instant tear the spear from the wood and be free to strike. But in that instant I ran in, and swinging my sword with all my great power, I hewed off his terrible head.

The heavings and contortions of Satha's prisoned form in life were naught to the convulsions of his headless length in death. I retreated, dragging the gigantic head after me with a crooked pole, and at a safe distance from the lashing, flying tail, I set to work. I worked with naked death then, and no man ever toiled more gingerly than did I. For I cut out the poison sacs at the base of the great fangs, and in the terrible venom I soaked the heads of eleven arrows, being careful that only the bronze points were in the liquid, which else had corroded away the wood of the tough shafts. While I was doing this, Grom, driven by comradeship and Curiosity, came stealing nervously through the jungle, and his mouth gaped as he looked on the head of Satha.

For hours I steeped the arrowheads in the poison, until they were caked with a horrible green scum, and showed tiny flecks of corrosion where the venom had eaten into the solid bronze. I wrapped them carefully in broad, thick, rubber-like leaves, and then, though night had fallen and the hunting beasts were roaring on every hand, I went back through the jungled hills, Grom with me, until at dawn we came again to the high cliffs that loomed above the Valley of Broken Stones.

At the mouth of the valley I broke my spear, and I took all the unpoisoned shafts from my quiver, and snapped them. I painted my face and limbs as the Æsir painted themselves only when they went forth to certain doom, and I sang my death-song to the sun as it rose over the cliffs, my yellow mane blowing in the morning wind.

Then I went down into the valley, bow in hand.

Grom could not drive himself to follow me. He lay on his belly in the dust and howled like a dying dog.

I passed the lake and the silent camp where the pyre-ashes still smoldered, and came under the thickening trees beyond. About me the columns loomed, mere shapeless heads from the ravages of Staggering aeons. The trees grew more dense, and under their vast leafy branches the very light was dusky and evil. As in twilight shadow I saw the ruined temple, cyclopean walls staggering up from masses of decaying masonry and fallen blocks of stone. About 600 yards in front of it a great column reared up in an open glade, 80 or 90 feet in height. It was so worn and pitted by weather and time that any child of my tribe could have climbed it, and I marked it and changed my plan.

I came to the ruins and saw huge crumbling walls upholding a domed roof from which many stones had fallen, so that it seemed like the lichen-grown ribs of some mythical monster's skeleton arching above me. Titanic columns flanked the open doorway through which ten elephants could have stalked abreast. Once there might have been inscriptions and hieroglyphics on the pillars and walls, but they were long worn away. Around the great room, on the inner side, ran columns in better state of preservation. On each of these columns was a flat pedestal, and some dim instinctive memory vaguely resurrected a shadowy scene wherein black drums roared madly, and on these pedestals monstrous beings squatted loathsomely in inexplicable rituals rooted in the black dawn of the universe.

There was no altar only the mouth of a great well-like shaft in the stone floor, with strange obscene carvings all about the rim. I tore great pieces of stone from the rotting floor and cast them down the shaft which slanted down into utter darkness. I heard them bound along the side, but I did not hear them strike bottom. I cast down stone after stone, each with a searing curse, and at last I heard a sound that was not the dwindling rumble of the falling stones. Up from the well floated a weird demon-piping that was a symphony of madness. Far down in the darkness I glimpsed the faint fearful glimmering of a vast white bulk.

I retreated slowly as the piping grew louder, falling back through the broad doorway. I heard a scratching, scrambling noise, and up from the shaft and out of the doorway between the colossal columns came a prancing incredible figure. It went erect like a man, but it was covered with fur, that was shaggiest where its face should have been. If it had ears, nose and a mouth I did not discover them. Only a pair of staring red eyes leered from the furry mask. Its misshapen hands held a strange set of pipes, on which it blew weirdly as it pranced towards me with many a grotesque caper and leap.

Behind it I heard a repulsive obscene noise as of a quaking unstable mass heaving up out of a well. Then I nocked an arrow, drew the cord and sent the shaft singing through the furry breast of the dancing monstrosity. It went down as though struck by a thunderbolt, but to my horror the piping continued, though the pipes had fallen from the malformed hands. Then I turned and ran fleetly to the column, up which I swarmed before I looked back. When I reached the pinnacle I looked, and because of the shock and surprise of what I saw, I almost fell from my dizzy perch.

Out of the temple the monstrous dweller in the darkness had come, and I, who had expected a horror yet cast in some terrestrial mould, looked on the spawn of nightmare. From what subterranean hell it crawled in the long ago I know not, nor what black age it represented. But it was not a beast, as humanity knows beasts. I call it a worm for lack of a better term. There is no earthly language that has a name for it. I can only say that it looked somewhat more like a worm than it did an octopus, a serpent or a dinosaur.

It was white and pulpy, and drew its quaking bulk along the ground, worm-fashion. But it had wide flat tentacles, and fleshy feelers, and other adjuncts the use of which I am unable to explain. And it had a long proboscis which it curled and uncurled like an elephant's trunk. Its forty eyes, set in a horrific circle, were composed of thousands of facets of as many scintillant colors which changed and altered in never-ending transmutation. But through all interplay of hue and glint, they retained their evil intelligence – intelligence there was behind those flickering facets, not human nor yet bestial, but a night-born demoniac intelligence such as men in dreams vaguely sense throbbing titanically in the black gulfs outside our material universe. In size the monster was mountainous; its bulk would have dwarfed a mastodon.

But even as I shook with the cosmic horror of the thing, I drew a feathered shaft to my ear and arched it singing on its way. Grass and bushes were crushed flat as the monster came towards me like a moving mountain and shaft after shaft I sent with terrific force and deadly precision. I could not miss so huge a target. The arrows sank to the feathers or clear out of sight in the unstable bulk, each bearing enough poison to have stricken dead a bull elephant. Yet on it came, swiftly, appallingly, apparently heedless of both the shafts and the venom in which they were steeped. And all the time the hideous music played a maddening accompaniment, whining thinly from the pipes that lay untouched on the ground.

My confidence faded; even the poison of Satha was futile against this uncanny being. I drove my last shaft almost straight downward into the quaking white mountain, so close was the monster under my perch. Then suddenly its color altered. A wave of ghastly blue surged over it, and the vast bulk heaved in earthquake-like convulsions. With a terrible plunge it struck the lower part of the column, which crashed to falling shards of stone. But even with the impact, I leaped far out and fell through the empty air full upon the monster's back.

The spongy skin yielded and gave beneath my feet, and I drove my sword hilt deep, dragging it through the pulpy flesh, ripping a horrible yard-long wound, from which oozed a green slime. Then a flip of a cable-like-tentacle flicked me from the titan's back and spun me 300 feet through the air to crash among a cluster of giant trees.

The impact must have splintered half the bones in my frame, for when I sought to grasp my sword again and crawl anew to the combat, I could not move hand or foot, could only writhe helplessly with my broken back. But I could see the monster and I knew that I had won, even in defeat. The mountainous bulk was heaving and billowing, the tentacles were lashing madly, the antennae writhing and knotting, and the nauseous whiteness had changed to a pale and grisly green. It turned ponderously and lurched back towards the temple, rolling like a crippled ship in a heavy swell. Trees crashed and splintered as it lumbered against them.

I wept with pure fury because I could not catch up my sword and rush in to die glutting my berserk madness in mighty strokes. But the worm-god was death-stricken and needed not my futile sword. The demon pipes on the ground kept up their infernal tune, and it was like the fiend's death-dirge. Then as the monster veered and floundered, I saw it catch up the corpse of its hairy slave. For an instant the apish form dangled in mid-air, gripped round by the trunk-like proboscis, then was dashed against the temple wall with a force that reduced the hairy body to a mere shapeless pulp. At that the pipes screamed out horribly, and fell silent for ever.

The titan staggered on the brink of the shaft; then another change came over it – a frightful transfiguration the nature of which I cannot yet describe. Even now when I try to think of it clearly, I am only chaotically conscious of a blasphemous, unnatural transmutation of form and substance, shocking and indescribable. Then the strangely altered bulk tumbled into the shaft to roll down into the ultimate darkness from whence it came, and I knew that it was dead. And as it vanished into the well, with a rending, grinding groan the ruined walls quivered from dome to base. They bent inward and buckled with deafening reverberation, the columns splintered, and with a cataclysmic crash the dome itself came thundering down. For an instant the air seemed veiled with flying debris and stone-dust, through which the treetops lashed madly as in a storm or an earthquake convulsion. Then all was clear again and I stared, shaking the blood from my eyes. Where the temple had stood there lay only a colossal pile of shattered masonry and broken stones, and every column in the valley had fallen, to lie in crumbling shards.

In the silence that followed I heard Grom wailing a dirge over me. I bade him lay my sword in my hand, and he did so, and bent close to hear what I had to say, for I was passing swiftly.

"Let my tribe remember," I said, speaking slowly. "Let the tale be told from village to village, from camp to camp, from tribe to tribe, so that men may know that not man nor beast nor devil may prey in safety on the golden-haired people of Asgard. Let them build me a cairn where I lie and lay me therein with my bow and sword at hand, to guard this valley for ever; so if the ghost of the god I slew comes up from below, my ghost will ever be ready to give it battle."

And while Grom howled and beat his hairy breast, death came to me in the Valley of the Worm.

The Garden of Fear

ONCE I WAS HUNWULF, THE WANDERER. I cannot explain my knowledge of this fact by any occult or esoteric means, nor shall I try. A man remembers his past life; I remember my past *lives*. Just as a normal individual recalls the shapes that were him in childhood, boyhood and youth, so I recall the shapes that have been James Allison in forgotten ages. Why this memory is mine I cannot say, any more than I can explain the myriad other phenomena of nature which daily confront me and every other mortal. But as I lie waiting for death to free me from my long disease, I see with a clear, sure sight the grand panorama of lives that trail out behind me. I see the men who have been me, and I see the beasts that have been me.

For my memory does not end at the coming of Man. How could it, when the beast so shades into Man that there is no clearly divided line to mark the boundaries of bestiality? At this instant I see a dim twilight vista, among the gigantic trees of a primordial forest that never knew the tread of a leather-shod foot. I see a vast, shaggy, shambling bulk that lumbers clumsily yet swiftly, sometimes upright, sometimes on all fours. He delves under rotten logs for grubs and insects, and his small ears twitch continually. He lifts his head and bares yellow fangs. He is primordial, bestial, anthropoid; yet I recognize his kinship with the entity now called James Allison. Kinship? Say rather oneness. I am he; he is I. My flesh is soft and white and hairless; his is dark and tough and shaggy. Yet we were one, and already in his feeble, shadowed brain are beginning to stir and tingle the man-thoughts and the man dreams, crude, chaotic, fleeting, yet the basis for all the high and lofty visions men have dreamed in all the following ages.

Nor does my knowledge cease there. It goes back, back, down immemorial vistas I dare not follow, to abysses too dark and awful for the human mind to plumb. Yet even there I am aware of my identity, my individuality. I tell you the individual is never lost, neither in the black pit from which we once crawled, blind, squalling and noisome, or in that eventual Nirvana in which we shall one day sink – which I have glimpsed afar off, shining as a blue twilight lake among the mountains of the stars.

But enough. I would tell you of Hunwulf. Oh, it was long, long ago! How long ago I dare not say. Why should I seek for paltry human comparisons to describe a realm indescribably, incomprehensibly distant? Since that age the earth had altered her contours not once but a dozen times, and whole cycles I of mankind have completed their destinies.

I was Hunwulf, a son of the golden-haired Æsir, who, from the icy plains of shadowy Asgard, sent I blue-eyed tribes around the world in century-long drifts to leave their trails in strange places. On one of those southward drifts I was born, for I never saw the homeland of my people, where the bulk of the Nordheimer still dwelt in their horse-hide tents among the snows.

I grew to manhood on that long wandering, to the fierce, sinewy, untamed manhood of the Æsir, who knew no gods but Ymir of the frost-rimmed beard, and whose axes are stained with the blood of many nations. My thews were like woven steel cords. My yellow hair fell in a lion-like mane to my mighty shoulders. My loins were girt with leopard skin. With either hand I could wield my heavy flint-headed axe. Year by year my tribe drifted southward, sometimes swinging in long arcs to east or west, sometimes lingering for months or years in fertile valleys or plains where the grass-eaters swarmed, but always forging slowly and inevitably southward. Sometimes our way led through vast and breathless solitudes that had never known a human cry; sometimes strange tribes disputed our course, and our trail passed over bloodstained ashes of butchered villages. And amidst this wandering, hunting and slaughtering, I came to full manhood and the love of Gudrun.

What shall I say of Gudrun? How describe color to the blind? I can say that her skin was whiter than milk, that her hair was living gold with the flame of the sun caught in it, that the supple beauty other body would shame the dream that shaped the Grecian goddesses. But I cannot make you realize the fire and wonder that was Gudrun. You have no basis for comparison; you know womanhood only by the women of your epoch, who, beside her are like candles beside the glow of the full moon. Not for a millennium of millenniums have women like Gudrun walked the earth. Cleopatra, Thais, Helen of Troy, they were but pallid shadows of her beauty, frail mimicries of the blossom that blooms to full glory only in the primordial.

For Gudrun I forsook my tribe and my people, and went into the wilderness, an exile and an outcast, with blood on my hands. She was of my race, but not of my tribe: a waif whom we found as a child wandering in a dark forest, lost from some wandering tribe of our blood. She grew up in the tribe, and when she came to the full ripeness of her glorious young womanhood, she was given to Heimdul the Strong, the mightiest hunter of the tribe.

But the dream of Gudrun was madness in my soul, a flame that burned eternally, and for her I slew Heimdul, crushing his skull with my flint-headed axe ere he could bear her to his horse-hide tent. And then follows our long flight from the vengeance of the tribe. Willingly she went with me, for she loved me with the love of the Æsir women, which is a devouring flame that destroys weakness. Oh, it was a savage age, when life was grim and bloodstained, and the weak died quickly. There was nothing mild or gentle about us, our passions were those of the tempest, the surge and impact of battle, the challenge of the lion. Our loves were as terrible as our hates.

And so I carried Gudrun from the tribe, and the killers were hot on our trail. For a night and a day they pressed us hard, until we swam a rising river, a roaring, foaming torrent that even the men of the Æsir dared not attempt. But in the madness of our love and recklessness we buffeted our way across, beaten and torn by the frenzy of the flood, and reached the farther bank alive.

Then for many days we traversed upland forests haunted by tigers and leopards, until we came to a great barrier of mountains, blue ramparts climbing awesomely to the sky. Slope piled upon slope.

In those mountains we were assailed by freezing winds and hunger, and by giant condors which swept down upon us with a thunder of gigantic wings. In grim battles in the passes I shot away all my arrows and splintered my flintheaded spear, but at last we crossed the bleak backbone of the range and descending the southern slopes, came upon a village of mud huts among the cliffs inhabited by a peaceful, brown-skinned people who spoke a strange tongue and had strange customs. But they greeted us with the sign of peace, and brought us into their village, where they set meat and barley-bread and fermented milk before us, and squatted in a ring about us while we ate, and a woman slapped softly on a bowl-shaped tom-tom to do us honor.

We had reached their village at dusk, and night fell while we feasted. On all sides rose the cliffs and peaks shouldering massively against the stars. The little cluster of mud huts and the tiny fires were drowned and lost in the immensity of the night. Gudrun felt the loneliness, the crowding desolation of that darkness, and she pressed close to me, her shoulder against my breast. But my axe was close at my hand, and I had never known the sensation of fear.

The little brown people squatted before us, men and women, and tried to talk to us with motions of their slender hands. Dwelling always in one place, in comparative security, they lacked both the strength and the uncompromising ferocity of the nomadic Æsir. Their hands fluttered with friendly gestures in the firelight.

I made them understand that we had come from the north, had crossed the backbone of the great mountain range, and that on the morrow it was our intention to descend into the green tablelands which we had glimpsed southward of the peaks. When they understood my meaning they set up a great cry shaking their heads violently, and beating madly on the drum. They were all so eager to impart something to me, and all waving their hands at once, that they bewildered rather than enlightened me. Eventually they did make me understand that they did not wish me to descend the mountains. Some menace lay to the south of the village, but whether of man or beast, I could not learn.

It was while they were all gesticulating and my whole attention was centered on their gestures, that the blow fell. The first intimation was a sudden thunder of wings in my ears; a dark shape rushed out of the night, and a great pinion dealt me a buffet over the head as I turned. I was knocked sprawling, and in that instant I heard Gudrun scream as she was torn from my side. Bounding up, quivering with a furious eagerness to rend and slay, I saw the dark shape vanish again into the darkness, a white, screaming, writhing figure trailing from its talons.

Roaring my grief and fury I caught up my axe and charged into the dark – then halted short, wild, desperate, knowing not which way to turn.

The little brown people had scattered, screaming, knocking sparks from their fires as they rushed over them in their haste to gain their huts, but now they crept out fearfully, whimpering like wounded dogs. They gathered around me and plucked at me with timid hands and chattered in their tongue while I cursed in sick impotency, knowing they wished to tell me something which I could not understand.

At last I suffered them to lead me back to the fire, and there the oldest man of the tribe brought forth a strip of cured hide, a clay pot of pigments, and a stick. On the hide he painted a crude picture of a winged thing carrying a white woman – oh, it was very crude, but I made out his meaning. Then all pointed southward and cried out loudly in their own tongue; and I knew that the menace they had warned me against was the thing that had carried off Gudrun. Until then I supposed that it had been one of the great mountain condors which had carried her away, but the picture the old man drew, in black paint, resembled a winging man more than anything else.

Then, slowly and laboriously, he began to trace something I finally recognized as a map – oh, yes, even in those dim days we had our primitive maps, though no modern man would be able to comprehend them so greatly different was our symbolism.

It took a long time; it was midnight before the old man had finished and I understood his tracings. But at last the matter was made clear. If I followed the course traced on the map, down the long narrow valley where stood the village, across a plateau, down a series of rugged slopes and along another valley, I would come to the place where lurked the being which had stolen my woman. At that spot the old man drew what looked like a misshapen hut, with many strange markings all about it in red pigments. Pointing to these, and again to me, he shook his head, with those loud cries that seemed to indicate peril among these people.

Then they tried to persuade me not to go, but afire with eagerness I took the piece of hide and pouch of food they thrust into my hands (they were indeed a strange people for that age), grasped my axe and set off in the moonless darkness. But my eyes were keener than a modern mind can comprehend, and my sense of direction was as a wolfs. Once the map was fixed in my mind, I could have thrown it away and come unerring to the place I sought but I folded it and thrust it into my girdle.

I traveled at my best speed through the starlight, taking no heed of any beasts that might be seeking their prey – cave bear or saber-toothed tiger. At times I heard gravel slide under stealthy padded paws; I glimpsed fierce yellow eyes burning in the darkness, and caught sight of shadowy, skulking forms. But I plunged on recklessly, in too desperate a mood to give the path to any beast however fearsome.

I traversed the valley, climbed a ridge and came out on a broad plateau, gashed with ravines and strewn with boulders. I crossed this and in the darkness before dawn commenced my climb down the treacherous slopes. They seemed endless, falling away in a long steep incline until their feet were lost in darkness. But I went down recklessly, not pausing to unsling the rawhide rope I carried about my shoulders, trusting to my luck and skill to bring me down without a broken neck.

And just as dawn was touching the peaks with a white glow, I dropped into a broad valley, walled by stupendous cliffs. At that point it was wide from east to west, but the cliffs converged toward the lower end, giving the valley the appearance of a great fan, narrowing swiftly toward the south.

The floor was level, traversed by a winding stream. Trees grew thinly; there was no underbrush, but a carpet of tall grass, which at that time of year were somewhat dry.

Along the stream where the green lush grew, wandered mammoths, hairy mountains of flesh and muscle.

I gave them a wide berth, giants too mighty for me to cope with, confident in their power, and afraid of only one thing on earth. They bent forward their great ears and lifted their trunks menacingly when I approached too near, but they did not attack me. I ran swiftly among the trees, and the sun was not yet above the eastern ramparts which its rising edged with golden flame, when I came to the point where the cliffs converged. My night-long climb had not affected my iron muscles. I felt no weariness; my fury burned unabated. What lay beyond the cliffs I could not know; I ventured no conjecture. I had room in my brain only for red wrath and killing-lust.

The cliffs did not form a solid wall. That is, the extremities of the converging palisades did not meet, leaving a notch or gap a few hundred feet wide, and emerged into a second valley, or rather into a continuance of the same valley which broadened out again beyond the pass.

The cliffs slanted away swiftly to east and west, to form a giant rampart that marched clear around the valley in the shape of a vast oval. It formed a blue rim all around the valley without a break except for a glimpse of the clear sky that seemed to mark another notch at the southern end. The inner valley was shaped much like a great bottle, with two necks.

The neck by which I entered was crowded with trees, which grew densely for several hundred yards, when they gave way abruptly to a field of crimson flowers. And a few hundred yards beyond the edges of the trees, I saw a strange structure.

I must speak of what I saw not alone as Hunwulf, but as James Allison as well. For Hunwulf only vaguely comprehended the things he saw, and, as Hunwulf, he could not describe them at all. I, as Hunwulf, knew nothing of architecture. The only man-built dwelling I had ever seen had been the horse-hide tents of my people, and the thatched mud huts of the barley people – and other people equally primitive.

So as Hunwulf I could only say that I looked upon a great hut the construction of which was beyond my comprehension. But I, James Allison, know that it was a tower, some seventy feet in height, of a curious green stone, highly polished, and of a substance that created the illusion of semi-translucency. It was cylindrical, and, as near as I could see, without doors or windows. The main body of the building was perhaps sixty feet in height, and from its center rose a smaller tower that completed its full stature. This tower, being much inferior in girth to the main body of the structure, and thus surrounded by a sort of gallery, with a crenellated parapet, and was furnished with both doors, curiously arched, and windows, thickly barred as I could see, even from where I stood.

That was all. No evidence of human occupancy. No sign of life in all the valley. But it was evident that this castle was what the old man of the mountain village had been trying to draw, and I was certain that in it I would find Gudrun – if she still lived.

Beyond the tower I saw the glimmer of a blue lake into which the stream, following the curve of the western wall, eventually flowed. Lurking amid the trees I glared at the tower and at the flowers surrounding it on all sides, growing thick along the walls and extending for hundreds of yards in all directions. There were trees at the other end of the valley, near the lake; but no trees grew among the flowers.

They were not like any plants I had ever seen. They grew close together, almost touching each other. They were some four feet in height, with only one blossom on each stalk, a blossom larger than a man's head, with broad, fleshy petals drawn close together. These petals were a livid crimson, the hue of an open wound. The stalks were thick as a man's wrist, colorless, almost transparent. The poisonously green leaves were shaped like spearheads, drooping on long snaky stems. Their whole aspect was repellent, and I wondered what their denseness concealed.

For all my wild-born instincts were roused in me. I felt lurking peril, just as I had often sensed the ambushed lion before my external senses recognized him. I scanned the dense blossoms closely, wondering if some great serpent lay coiled among them. My nostrils expanded as I quested for a scent, but the wind was blowing away from me. But there was something decidedly unnatural about that vast garden. Though the north wind swept over it, not a blossom stirred, not a leaf rustled; they hung motionless, sullen, like birds of prey with drooping heads, and I had a strange feeling that they were watching me like living things.

It was like a landscape in a dream: on either hand the blue cliffs lifting against the cloud-fleeced sky; in the distance the dreaming lake; and that fantastic green tower rising in the midst of that livid crimson field.

And there was something else: in spite of the wind that was blowing away from me, I caught a scent, a charnel-house reek of death and decay and corruption that rose from the blossoms.

Then suddenly I crouched closer in my covert. There was life and movement on the castle. A figure emerged from the tower, and coming to the parapet, leaned upon it and looked out across the valley. It was a man, but such a man as I had never dreamed of, even in nightmares.

He was tall, powerful, black with the hue of polished ebony; but the feature which made a human nightmare of him was the batlike wings which folded on his shoulders. I knew they were wings: the fact was obvious and indisputable.

I, James Allison, have pondered much on that phenomenon which I witnessed through the eyes of Hunwulf. Was that winged man merely a freak, an isolated example of distorted nature, dwelling in solitude and immemorial desolation? Or was he a survival of a forgotten race, which had risen, reigned and vanished before the coming of man as we know him? The little brown people of the hills might have told me, but we had no speech in common. Yet I am inclined to the latter theory. Winged men are not uncommon in mythology; they are met with in the folklore of many nations and many races. As far back as man may go in myth, chronicle and legend, he finds tales of harpies and winged gods, angels and demons. Legends are distorted shadows of pre-existent realities, I believe that once a race of winged black men ruled a pre-Adamite world, and that I, Hunwulf, met the last survivor of that race in the valley of the red blossoms.

These thoughts I think as James Allison, with my modern knowledge which is as imponderable as my modern ignorance.

I, Hunwulf, indulged in no such speculations. Modern skepticism was not a part of my nature, nor did I seek to rationalize what seemed not to coincide with a natural universe. I acknowledged no gods but Ymir and his daughters, but I did not doubt the existence – as demons – of other deities, worshipped by other races. Supernatural beings of all sorts fitted into my conception of life and the universe. I no more doubted the existence of dragons, ghosts, fiends and devils than I doubted the existence of lions and buffaloes and elephants. I accepted this freak of nature as a supernatural demon and did not worry about its origin or source. Nor was I thrown into a panic of superstitious fear. I was a son of Asgard, who feared neither man nor devil, and I had more faith in the crushing power of my flint axe than in the spells of priests or the incantations of sorcerers.

But I did not immediately rush into the open and charge the tower. The wariness of the wild was mine, and I saw no way to climb the castle. The winged man needed no doors on the side, because he evidently entered at the top, and the slick surface of the walls seemed to defy the most skillful climber. Presently a way of getting upon the tower occurred to me, but I hesitated, waiting to see if any other winged people appeared, though I had an unexplainable feeling that he was the only one of his kind in the valley – possibly in the world. While I crouched among the trees and watched, I saw him lift his elbows from the parapet and stretch lithely, like a great cat. Then he strode across the circular gallery and entered the tower. A muffled cry rang out on the air which caused me to stiffen, though even so I realized that it was not the cry of a woman. Presently the black master of the castle emerged, dragging a smaller figure with him – a figure which writhed and struggled and cried out piteously. I saw that it was a small brown man, much like those of the mountain village. Captured, I did not doubt, as Gudrun had been captured.

He was like a child in the hands of his huge foe. The black man spread broad wings and rose over the parapet, carrying his captive as a condor might carry a sparrow. He soared out over the field of blossoms, while I crouched in my leafy retreat, glaring in amazement.

The winged man, hovering in mid-air, voiced a strange weird cry; and it was answered in horrible fashion. A shudder of awful life passed over the crimson field beneath him. The great red blossoms trembled, opened, spreading their fleshy petals like the mouths of serpents. Their stalks seemed to elongate, stretching upward eagerly. Their broad leaves lifted and vibrated with a curious lethal whirring, like the singing of a rattlesnake. A faint but flesh-crawling hissing sounded over all the valley. The blossoms gasped, straining upward. And with a fiendish laugh, the winged man dropped his writhing captive.

With a scream of a lost soul the brown man hurtled downward, crashing among the flowers. And with a rustling hiss, they were on him. Their thick flexible stalks arched like the necks of serpents, their petals closed on his flesh. A hundred blossoms clung to him like the tentacles of an octopus, smothering and crushing him down. His shrieks of agony came muffled; he was completely hidden by the hissing, threshing flowers. Those beyond reach swayed and writhed furiously as if seeking to tear up their roots in their eagerness to join their brothers. All over the field the great red blossoms leaned and strained toward the spot where the grisly battle went on. The shrieks sank lower and lower and lower, and ceased. A dread silence reigned over the valley. The black man flapped his way leisurely back to the tower, and vanished within it.

Then presently the blossoms detached themselves one by one from their victim who lay very white and still. Aye, his whiteness was more than that of death; he was like a wax image, a staring effigy from which every drop of blood had been sucked. And a startling transmutation was evident in the flowers directly about him. Their stalks no longer colorless; they were swollen and dark red, like transparent bamboos filled to the bursting with fresh blood.

Drawn by an insatiable curiosity, I stole from the trees and glided to the very edge of the red field. The blossoms hissed and bent toward me, spreading their petals like the hood of a roused cobra. Selecting one farthest from its brothers, I severed the stalk with a stroke of my axe, and the thing tumbled to the ground, writhing like a beheaded serpent.

When its struggles ceased I bent over it in wonder. The stalk was not hollow as I had supposed – that is, hollow like a dry bamboo. It was traversed by a network of thread-like veins, some empty and some exuding a colorless sap. The stems which held the leaves to the stalk were remarkably tenacious and pliant, and the leaves themselves were edged with curved spines, like sharp hooks.

Once those spines were sunk in the flesh, the victim would be forced to tear up the whole plant by the roots if he escaped.

The petals were each as broad as my hand, and as thick as a prickly pear, and on the inner side covered with innumerable tiny mouths, not larger than the head of a pin. In the center, where the pistil should be, there was a barbed spike, of a substance like thorn, and narrow channels between the four serrated edges.

From my investigations of this horrible travesty of vegetation, I looked up suddenly, just in time to see the winged man appear again on the parapet. He did not seem particularly surprised to see me. He shouted in his unknown tongue and made a mocking gesture, while I stood statue-like, gripping my axe. Presently he turned and entered the tower as he had done before; and as before, he emerged with a captive. My fury and hate were almost submerged by the flood of joy that Gudrun was alive.

In spite of her supple strength, which was that of a she-panther, the black man handled Gudrun as easily as he had handled the brown man. Lifting her struggling white body high above his head, he displayed her to me and yelled tauntingly. Her golden hair streamed over her white shoulders as she fought vainly, crying to me in the terrible extremity of her fright and horror. Not lightly was a woman of the Æsir reduced to cringing terror. I measured the depths of her captor's diabolism by her frenzied cries.

But I stood motionless. If it would have saved her, I would have plunged into that crimson morass of hell, to be hooked and pierced and sucked white by those fiendish flowers. But that would help her none. My death would merely leave her without a defender. So I stood silent while she writhed and whimpered, and the black man's laughter sent red waves of madness surging across my brain. Once he made as if to cast her down among the flowers, and my iron control almost snapped and sent me plunging into that red sea of hell. But it was only a gesture. Presently he dragged her back to the tower and tossed her inside. Then he turned back to the parapet, rested his elbows upon it, and fell to watching me. Apparently he was playing with us as a cat plays with a mouse before he destroys it.

But while he watched, I turned my back and strode into the forest. I, Hunwulf, was not a thinker, as modern men understand the term. I lived in an age where emotions were translated by the smash of a flint axe rather than by emanations of the intellect. Yet I was not the senseless animal the black man evidently supposed me to be. I had a human brain, whetted by the eternal struggle for existence and supremacy.

I knew I could not cross that red strip that banded the castle, alive. Before I could take a half dozen steps a score of barbed spikes would be thrust into my flesh, their avid mouths sucking the flood from my veins to feed their demoniac lust. Even my tigerish strength would not avail to hew a path through them.

The winged man did not follow. Looking back, I saw him still lounging in the same position. When I, as James Allison, dream again the dreams of Hunwulf, that, image is etched in my mind, that gargoyle figure with elbows propped on the parapet, like a medieval devil brooding on the battlements of hell.

I passed through the straits of the valley and came into the vale beyond where the trees thinned and the mammoths lumbered along the stream. Beyond the herd I stopped and drawing a pair of flints into my pouch, stooped and struck a spark in the dry grass. Running swiftly from chosen place to place, I set a dozen fires, in a great semi-circle. The north wind caught them, whipped them into eager life, drove them before it. In a few moments a rampart of flame was sweeping down the valley.

The mammoths ceased their feeding, lifted their great ears and bellowed alarm. In all the world they feared only fire. They began to retreat southward, the cows herding the calves before them, bulls trumpeting like the blast of Judgement Day. Roaring like a storm the fire rushed on, and the mammoths broke and stampeded, a crushing hurricane of flesh, a thundering earthquake of hurtling bone and muscle. Trees splintered and went down before them, the ground shook under their headlong tread. Behind them came the racing fire and on the heels of the fire came I, so closely that the smoldering earth burnt the moose-hide sandals off my feet.

Through the narrow neck they thundered, leveling the dense thickets like a giant scythe. Trees were torn up by the roots; it was as if a tornado had ripped through the pass.

With a deafening thunder of pounding feet and trumpeting, they stormed across the sea of red blossoms. Those devilish plants might have even pulled down and destroyed a single mammoth; but under the impact of the whole herd, they were no more than common flowers. The maddened titans crashed through and over them, battering them to shreds, hammering, stamping them into the earth which grew soggy with their juice.

I trembled for an instant, fearing the brutes would not turn aside for the castle, and dubious of even it being able to withstand that battering ram concussion. Evidently the winged man shared my fears, for he shot up from the tower and raced off through the sky toward the lake. But one of the bulls butted head-on into the wall, was shunted off the smooth curving surface, caromed into the one next to him, and the herd split and roared by the tower on either hand, so closely their hairy sides rasped against it. They thundered on through the red field toward the distant lake.

The fire, reaching the edge of the trees, was checked; the smashed sappy fragments of the red flowers would not burn. Trees, fallen or standing, smoked and burst into flame, and burning branches showered around me as I ran through the trees and out into the gigantic swath the charging herd had cut through the livid field.

As I ran I shouted to Gudrun and she answered me. Her voice was muffled and accompanied by a hammering on something. The winged man had locked her in a tower.

As I came under the castle wall, treading on remnants of red petals and snaky stalks, I unwound my rawhide rope, swung it, and sent its loop shooting upward to catch on one of the merlons of the crenellated parapet. Then I went up it, hand over hand, gripping the rope between my toes, bruising my knuckles and elbows against the sheer wall as I swung about.

I was within five feet of the parapet when I was galvanized by the beat of wings about my head. The black man shot out of the air and landed on the gallery. I got a good look at him as he leaned over the parapet. His features were straight and regular; there was no suggestion of the negroid about him. His eyes were slanted slits, and his teeth gleamed in a savage grin of hate and triumph. Long, long he had ruled the valley of the red blossoms, leveling tribute of human lives from the miserable tribes of the hills, for writhing victims to feed the carnivorous half-bestial flowers which were his subjects and protectors. And now I was in his power, my fierceness, and craft gone for naught. A stroke of the crooked dagger in his hand and I would go hurtling to my death. Somewhere Gudrun, seeing my peril, was screaming like a wild thing, and then a door crashed with a splintering of wood.

The black man, intent upon his gloating, laid the keen edge of his dagger on the rawhide strand – then a strong white arm locked about his neck from behind, and he was jerked violently backward. Over his shoulder I saw the beautiful face of Gudrun, her hair standing on end, her eyes dilated with terror and fury.

With a roar he turned in her grasp, tore loose her clinging arms and hurled her against the tower with such force that she lay half stunned. Then he turned again to me, but in that instant I had swarmed up and over the parapet, and leaped upon the gallery, unslinging my axe.

For an instant he hesitated, his wings half-lifted, his hand poising on his dagger, as if uncertain whether to fight or take to the air. He was a giant in stature, with muscles standing out in corded ridges all over him, but he hesitated, as uncertain as a man when confronted by a wild beast.

I did not hesitate. With a deep-throated roar I sprang, swinging my axe with all my giant strength. With a strangled cry he threw up his arms; but down between them the axe plunged and blasted his head to red ruin.

I wheeled toward Gudrun; and struggling to her knees, she threw her white arms about me in a desperate clasp of love and terror, staring awedly to where lay the winged lord of the valley, the crimson pulp that had been his head drowned in a puddle of blood and brains.

I had often wished that it were possible to draw these various lives of mine together in one body, combining the experiences of Hunwulf with the knowledge of James Allison. Could that be so, Hunwulf would have gone through the ebony door which Gudrun in her desperate strength had shattered, into that weird chamber he glimpsed through the ruined panels, with fantastic furnishing, and shelves heaped with rolls of parchment. He would have unrolled those scrolls and pored over their characters until he deciphered them, and read, perhaps, the chronicles of that weird race whose last survivor he had just slain. Surely the tale was stranger than an opium dream, and marvelous as the story of lost Atlantis.

But Hunwulf had no such curiosity. To him the tower, the ebony furnished chamber and the rolls of parchment were meaningless, inexplicable emanations of sorcery, whose significance lay only in their diabolism. Though the solution of mystery lay under his fingers, he was a far removed from it as James Allison, millenniums yet unborn.

To me, Hunwulf, the castle was but a monstrous trap, concerning which I had but one emotion, and that a desire to escape from it as quickly as possible.

With Gudrun clinging to me I slid to the ground, then with a dexterous flip I freed my rope and wound it; and after that we went hand and hand along the path made by the mammoths, now vanishing in the distance, toward the blue lake at the southern end of the valley and the notch in the cliffs beyond it.

Other Robert Howard works from Benediction Classics

'The Weird Menace Collection' showcases Howard's horror stories and comprises the four 'Weird Menace' books: Black Talons, Moon of Zambebwei, Skull-Face and Black Wind Blowing

ISBN: 978-1-84902-450-1

A Western adventure from Howard about a bank robbery that goes badly wrong, leading to a ferocious chase for the culprits.

ISBN: 978-1-84902-736-6

A work of semi-historical fiction that introduces Howard's celebrated swords-woman, Red Sonya of Rogatino.

ISBN: 978-1-84902-561-4

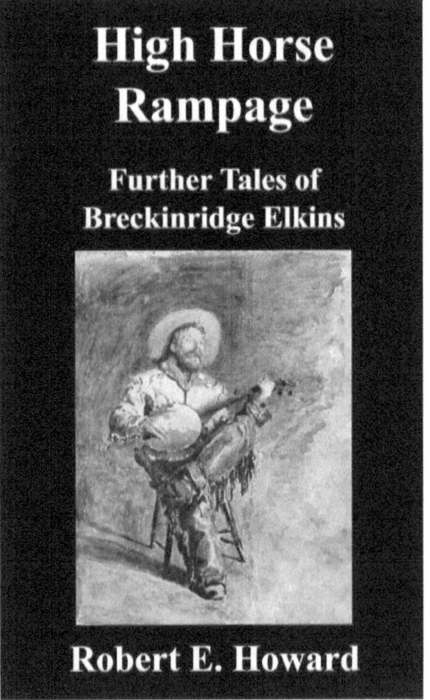

High Horse Rampage: the further Tales of Breckinridge Elkins puts Howard's comic Western hero into more adventures, fist-fights and gun battles.

ISBN: 978-1-84902-692-5

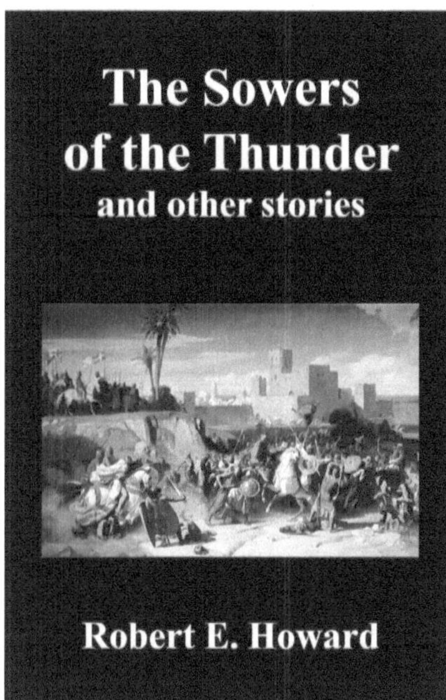

A collection of four of Robert Howard's Historical Adventures: The Sowers of the Thunder , Gates of Empire, Lord of Samarcand, and The Lion of Tiberias.

ISBN: 978-1-84902-729-8

Stories featuring Howard's 17th century puritan hero: Skulls in the Stars, The Footfalls Within, The Moon of Skulls, The Hills of the Dead,Wings in the Night, Rattle of Bones and Red Shadows

ISBN: 978-1-84902-732-8

www.ingramcontent.com/pod-product-compliance
Lightning Source LLC
Chambersburg PA
CBHW030342310726
48979CB00001B/157

* 9 7 8 1 8 4 9 0 2 3 5 3 5 *